# Snowball

## Watch Out!
## Light and Dark Stories for the Season

By
*Jennifer U.Egan*
*G.Z. Hill*
*Stephanie Raffelock*

# Dedication

*To all women*
*who write and share their voice.*

# Contents

# Uh, Oh, Christmas Tree

*By Jennifer U. Egan*

Karen's husband Todd already had the windshield wipers turned on low when she got in with the backpack and slammed the door of the pickup. She liked the sound of the wipers back and forth as they whisked the large snowflakes away.

"Can't you close the door without slamming so hard?"

Her back stiffened as she avoided looking at him. She turned and looked behind his seat.

"Do you have the ax and saw?"

"Of course I have the ax and saw. What a stupid question."

"You forgot them that one year."

"That was five years ago! Why do you always bring that up?"

He put the truck in reverse and slid a bit as he backed up.

"It's starting to snow pretty hard now. It will probably be snowing a lot harder up there and it will be dark soon."

"Look do you want a tree or not? I'm not going up on Saturday."

—
9

"Okay, okay let's go." She looked away from him.

He started down the driveway before she fastened her seatbelt.

"Hey wait a minute."

He kept driving not looking at her. She could tell he just wanted to get this over with.

They hardly passed any cars. Most people wouldn't go out on a night like this to get a Christmas tree. Most people would wait till a sunny afternoon and make more fun out of it.

They took the turn up Dead Indian Memorial road. They left behind houses with Christmas lights along their roofs and curved up the road into a more rural area. Houses were further apart here. Sometimes you could only see the beginnings of long driveways from the road.

"Did you get a permit?" she asked.

"No."

"You should've gotten a permit. It's only five bucks and makes it legal."

"We're not going to a designated cutting area."

"You mean we're going to cut a tree off someone's private land again. I hate that."

"I hate that." He imitated her and laughed. "God you're stupid. It saves money plus we have four-wheel drive. I can handle driving off the road."

"You're going to get caught some time."

"Hey, one good reason that it's snowing," he laughed again. "No one will see us."

"I wish you'd gotten a permit. What are you going to use the extra money for, beer?"

"What do you want it to buy something for the kids? That's what you always do."

Karen's hands played with the seat belt. It seemed tighter than usual. The truck seemed too small inside. She wished they'd get there. She wanted this over with. The snow was coming down hard now. He should turn the wipers up faster but she didn't want to say it and be yelled at again. The driveways were getting farther and farther apart and soon they would turn out into the woods where there was no one for miles. It didn't feel safe. There was no cell phone reception out there. What if they got stuck?

"Do we really want a tree this year?" she asked.

"What?" He looked at her like she was crazy.

"The kids aren't coming again."

"We always have a Christmas tree."

"I don't know that it's fun without the kids. Maybe we should just turn around."

His fingers tightened on the steering wheel.

She turned the windshield wipers up to high speed.

His jaw tightened and he jutted his face at her. "Hey who's driving?"

"This is the third year they haven't come is all. Maybe they don't want to come."

"God you're stupid. They're grown now."

He kept driving and they were quiet.

"I brought a Christmas CD. You want to listen to it?"

"No. I just want to focus on the road and get the damned tree."

A couple minutes later he slowed and took a left up a long drive. It was beginning to get dark and he had the car's headlights on high. No houses up here. He drove in for about ten miles.

"Hey, we don't usually drive in this far."

"Yeah I wanted to try a new place. There's no one here. Its just land owned by some Californians."

He stopped the truck and put the emergency brake on. "You get the ax and I'll start looking."

"We'd better hurry. It's getting dark and there's no moon tonight."

"You're so weak. Just leave the lights on high beam."

Todd was out of the pickup and walking straight ahead. He was carrying the saw and the ropes to pull the tree back to the truck.

Karen laced up her boots and put the ax in her backpack with the thermos. She hoped that he wouldn't choose one too far away. Her back hurt sometimes now and she didn't want to help pull one too far. The sun was almost all the way down when she opened her door and got out. It wasn't good being up here alone like this, not safe. She was glad that she'd taken the time to put on double socks. Her feet were warm inside the rubber-soled boots. She loved the half squashing, half squeaking sound this deeper snow made as she walked in it.

Karen remembered her kids loving these trips when they were little. She'd carried coco in the thermos in those days. The snowy world had been a playground for them. When her three kids were little they couldn't wait to get out and run, never walk, not at first anyway, no run in this cold white landscape. Laughter was in her thoughts with those memories and she caught herself smiling. Snow throwing and then snowman building merrily on until finally with a tree secured on top of the pickup, Todd was yelling for them to all get in the truck NOW!"

"We're taking this one. Hurry up with the AX!"

God, he seemed a long ways from the truck. The snow was getting deeper and she walked towards him but it was difficult to go fast. She finally reached him. She took off her backpack and took out the ax and handed it to him.

"Watch out."

He started to chop at the base of the tree.

She wondered if it were harder to cut because it was freezing. Even with her extra socks her toes were feeling the dropping temperature.

"I think the trunk is too big. It might not fit in the stand."

"Shut up. Just shut up and get me some coffee. I've already started and this is the one we're getting."

She took the thermos from the pack and poured coffee in a cup. She handed it to him. He took a swig and threw the cup at her. In the beams from the pickup lights she saw the stain of the coffee in the snow.

"Shit. Where is the cream and sugar? I hate it black. You know that."

She was quiet. She took the cup and the thermos and put them in the pack and then headed back towards the truck.

"And make it double cream," he yelled after her.

He returned to chopping at the stubborn trunk.

She got to the car and opened the passenger door. She put the thermos on the seat and closed the door. She went around to the driver's side and got in. The keys were still in the ignition. Through the thick snow she could see him chopping the tree, the green limbs wrestling with him as he brought the ax in and out. Karen put the truck in drive and pulled forward a bit and then turned it around. He looked up when he saw the taillights going down the long drive.

"Hey!" He hit his head on one of the limbs. The lights grew dimmer as the truck pulled away.

Karen drove carefully down the road. The pickup had snow tires but you never knew when you might hit an ice patch. Once she turned onto Dead Indian Memorial road again only a couple of cars passed her as she headed home. No one was coming down with trees. It was dark now and the temperature was dropping. It was a dumb time to be out getting a tree. She came to the end the road where it joined the old highway. She turned right toward the freeway instead of left toward home. Merging onto I-5 she noticed that a line of trucks was backed up on the southbound side waiting to get over the pass. On the northbound side to Medford traffic was moving.

She took the first Medford exit and drove to the seedy downtown area. She parked the truck in front of a strip joint, turned it off but left the keys in the ignition. Karen walked until she was near the Red Lion Hotel. She took out her cell phone and started to call a taxi but then saw that one was parked in front of the hotel just unloading someone's luggage.

"Are you available?"

"I will be in a minute. Where are you headed?"

"I need a ride just out past Ashland."

"You got it. Go ahead and get in."

She asked to be taken to the Glenyan Campground near Emigrant Lake.

"You from around here?"

"No. I'm just visiting my sister."

At first the cabbie talked but she gave only short answers and he stopped. She wanted to be quiet.

When they got to the trailer park she unzipped her jacket pocket to get her wallet. She gave him a twenty and told him to keep the change. Then she walked the mile to her home. She had the small flashlight she always kept in her pocket and tonight she needed it. There were also some house lights still on along the way.

She reached their home and unlocked the front door. Walking through the quiet she crossed the room to the phone. The message machine light was flashing. She stopped breathing and pressed the button.

A woman's voice said, "If you would like to receive information on re-mortgaging your home…"

Karen pressed the erase button and released the air from her lungs.

The wood stove was still warm. She opened the cast iron door and put two more logs on. She left the door open so the blast of warmth would fill the room. She walked to the kitchen and got a glass of water. Slowly she drank, drinking and pausing to hold the glass and then drinking the rest. She went back to the couch and sat, coat still on, staring at the blaze. The red and gold flames reached out and then pulled back. It was some kind of dance she was watching, as the wood got smaller. She sat in the dark, in the quiet. She waited. Just after ten she got up and turned the light on. She went to the phone and called the police.

"Ashland Police department, how may I help you?"

"I am calling because my husband went up to get a Christmas tree and he hasn't come home yet."

"Where did he go?"

"I don't know."

"Do you know the general area he went to?"

"No. I have no idea. Somewhere up Dead Indian Memorial I think."

"It's snowing hard up there now Ma'am and it's supposed to be one of the coldest nights of the year." The line was quiet and then he added, "I'll let the forest rangers know but we can't send people out till tomorrow. They'll need to know what general area he went to."

---

16

"He just drove off and didn't tell me."

Karen gave her name and her information to the officer.

"Well let us know if he gets home."

"I will," she said and then hung up.


The next day an officer came out to ask more questions.

They didn't find Todd after a search involving numerous people. They did find his stolen truck. Some drunk had been stopped for a DUI while driving it. They stopped looking for Todd in the woods after that.

∎∎∎∎∎∎∎∎∎∎∎∎∎∎∎∎∎∎∎∎∎∎∎∎∎∎∎∎∎∎∎∎∎∎∎∎∎∎∎∎∎∎∎∎∎∎∎∎∎∎∎∎∎

Karen waited for a beautiful day in July, a sunny gorgeous day. She curled her hair and put on a dress. She grabbed her backpack putting it on the passenger seat next to her. They had returned the truck to her and she was glad since she might need the four-wheel drive. She drove out of the driveway and headed towards Dead Indian Memorial road. Warm air wafted in both windows. She was surprised how easily she found the drive. She turned left into it and headed up watching to see when she had driven in close to ten miles. She kept going up a little further. It was steep going in. Then she saw it. The pine with dead needles now. She parked the truck and got out taking her backpack with her. She walked towards the tree. It was funny he had dragged it a bit toward where the car had been.

"You thought I was coming back." She said out loud. She looked around and didn't see him. This gave her a chill. Had he walked out? It had been so cold. She walked around looking for any clue. No footprints. Those would've disappeared as snow melted long ago. Then she saw something red. She quickened her pace and walked towards it but then pulled back. There were bones and still some flesh with pieces of his coat around. Had the animal eaten him after he was gone from cold? She'd probably never know. Karen took off her backpack and opened it. She crouched next to what was left of him. She felt calm near him now. Bones couldn't yell. First she opened the baggie of sugar and dusted what was left of him and lastly she unscrewed the small jar and slowly poured the white liquid over him as well.

"You did say you wanted double cream didn't you?"

She screwed the top back on the jar, put everything back into her pack and returned to her truck. She turned it around and headed back toward the main road and home.

# Rush

*By Jennifer U. Egan*

"Tammy, you are saying you don't want me to come for Christmas?"

"Oh God Annette, we'll have a house full. You know that, the kids, the grandkids. Besides it didn't go well the last time remember?"

"That was five years ago."

"Yes we remember," said Tammy.

"Didn't they like their presents then?"

"Annette, forget the damned stuff it's not about the stuff. Get it? Why don't you just come up for a couple days after the holiday? We can go to lunch."

"I can't afford it."

There was a silence and then, "I thought you just said you wanted to come up for the holidays."

"I really just don't have the money Tammy."

"You could afford to come up if you didn't buy all that junk."

"Why don't you come down?"

"And where would we stay Annette? Where? You can't even walk through your hallway!"

Annette could hear Tammy's husband in the background.

"Tammy we're meeting the kids for breakfast. Let's go."

"Look I got to go. Thanks for calling. Look Annette, we don't want any stuff. Don't send anything. Goodbye."

Annette gripped her home phone receiver hard and then slammed it down when she heard the dial tone. Thankless sister. Thankless ungrateful nieces and nephews, she had often sent them presents. Well, she hadn't for about five years now. So what? Nieces and nephews or not, sister or no sister she still had shopping to do.

Annette shopped religiously every weekend. And she was amazingly organized about it. Already dressed, Annette turned sideways so that she could make her way past the piled boxes to the bathroom. She took out her curlers and combed her short now graying hair. She picked up the large can of super hold hairspray but nothing came out when she pressed the top button. No worries. She placed the can in the white plastic bathroom wastebasket and walked back down the hallway sideways to the linen closet. She pushed the tall pile of new beach towels to the side.

"Oh Tammy, your family has no idea what they're missing. So many gifts," she said out loud.

She was able to open the closet door part way and she smiled broadly at what she saw, five new cans of hairspray.

"I am not a woman of want that is for sure."

She grabbed one can, shut the closet door and made her way back to her bathroom.

Once there she sprayed her short, now curly locks. Next she opened a drawer to reveal no less than forty assorted lipsticks of varying colors. She rifled through them and stopped at a bright shiny red one. She picked it up and looked at the bottom label.

"*Cranberry Red*! Just the one for holiday shopping."

She opened the tube and pulled out the brush and painted her lips. Twisting the tube shut she dropped it into her purse, which was sitting on the counter.

She took out her wallet and checked to make sure she had her credit cards. It gave her pleasure to count all twenty of them. She had such good credit. She always paid the minimum amount on time. It allowed her the freedom of so much buying power.

In her excitement to get going she knocked down a couple stacks of folded shopping bags in the foyer. She took the time to pick them up and return them to their tower. Annette was a person of order after all. She so favored these lovely paper bags over the plastic ones. She had saved quite a few over the years.

Yes, Annette had accumulated and organized so many items. Even if she stopped purchasing things now she would probably have enough clothing for the rest of her life; sweaters, pants and dresses, styles changed but then the styles returned right? Even though she never cooked she was well set with cooking ware. She also had stacks of sheets and comforters. She had saved so much on everything, a fortune really.

Shopping bags neatly back in place, leaning against the wall; she opened her front door and locked it behind her. Annette climbed into her twelve-year-old Ford and was off to the mall. On the drive there she always took the same roads to the freeway. It was through a poorer section of town and she made sure her car doors were securely locked as she passed by the houses with peeling paint and the dirty children playing in the front yards. Most of these homes didn't even put up Christmas decorations. Missing life, that's what they were doing. She on the other hand had a garage full of outdoor light up ornaments and tree decorations.

Entering the mall, holiday music massaged her eardrums. This year they had plastic reindeer flying over the food court and giant gold ball ornaments gracing the mall center. *Good job* she thought. *Thank God for Macy's, Kohl's, JC Penney's and the other retailers.* She was sure that they must combine their efforts with regards to the mall decorations.

Annette walked about window-shopping at first and then began pulling out her multiple charge cards to make purchases. First she bought placemats at Kohl's where they were having a killer sale. *You could never have too many of those.* Next she headed to Macy's and went directly to the 70% off clothing rack. *Who would ever buy full price? Only someone stupid would pay full price.* One pocket of her purse was filled with coupons, which made it even better. She made a pile of clothing on the floor near her and looked at pants and tops adding to the pile until she had about twenty items. Then she headed to the dressing room to try everything on. (True some of the pants were a little big but didn't people gain weight, as they got older? That could happen. She'd be ready.) She carried her choices to the cashier and using her 20% coupon on top of the 70% discount, made her purchases.

The sales woman handed her two paper shopping bags filled with her new clothing. *OH, her favorite kind of bag!* She held one in each hand and enjoyed the feel of the roped paper handles. A shiver went up her arms and into her abdomen. She had what she guessed was an almost sexual feeling. Ah, such pleasure.

She walked towards the exit doors and was shocked to see snow falling heavily. She glanced at her watch and saw that it was close to five o'clock. She had been enjoying her day so much that she had lost track of time. Unfortunately she had also forgotten where she had parked. Most of the cars in the parking lot were all covered in snow. Some, hers included probably, had an inch or two on their hood and roofs.

"Don't Panic," Annette said to herself. "I will just walk up and down until I find my car."

And so she began. Annette walked up and down two complete rows of cars. She was wearing short heels, which were buried in the snow with each step. She felt the wet, cold melt on her feet. Feeling chilled she set her shopping bags down to button her coat. She walked down another row. Annette heard ripping sounds. A pile of new pants and tops dropped onto the snow covered ground."

"No, no, no!" She yelled.

A short woman who was just getting out of her car walked over to her. "Are you alright?"

"Yes. I mean no. My bag just broke and I can't find my car," said Annette. She looked more closely at the woman's face. "You look familiar."

The woman looked at her, "Oh you do too. Do you have a white Ford?"

"Yes, that's what I am looking for right now," said Annette.

"Oh, I think maybe I've seen you driving by my house on Lark Street, maybe even this morning? Are we neighbors?"

"Oh Lark street, yes. I drive down that street on my way to the freeway."

"I'm Elena Rodriguez. It is so cold. Why don't you get in my car and we'll drive up and down the rows to look for your car."

"No, I …"

"Otherwise you're going to have a hard time carrying all those things."

It was true. Some of her new purchases were already wet and dirty.

"Well okay. Thank you."

Elena opened the passenger door and Annette got in. There was some kind of stuffed bear toy on the car floor in front of her and a baby seat minus the baby strapped in the back.

"You have children?"

"Yes, three, a five-year-old boy and then two little girls. And you? And what did you say your name was?"

"I didn't but my name is Annette. No, no children. But nieces and nephews yes."

"Annette. Maybe we should open our windows to look for your car."

"Okay." Annette lowered her slightly fogged up window. Slowly they went up and down the rows. On the fifth row Annette said, "Wait, wait. I think that's it. Stop please."

Elena stopped and Annette got out. She wiped some snow off the car's window and inside she saw her blue umbrella. Thank God she thought.

"This is it!" said Annette. "Thank you so much."

"Here let me help you put your things in the car." Elena stopped her car and together they loaded all of Annette's purchases into her trunk.

Annette started to get in her car but then stopped and turned around. "Isn't yours the house with the tire swing in the front yard?"

"Yes that's right."

"Yes, I have seen you and your family."

"Well I am going to go park and shop. Alfredo is at home and this is my shopping time without the children."

"Oh of course. Thank you Elena."

"You are welcome Annette. Nice to meet you. Drive carefully."

"Annette smiled and watched as Elena drove away in search of another parking spot."

On the drive home Annette was scared. Yesterday's evening news had not even mentioned a possibility of snow. This must've been some unexpected freak storm. She took the old highway route avoiding the freeway. What a traumatic day this had been. First this awful storm, forgetting where she was parked and then the bag ripping. Something else horrible might happen. Bad things happened in bunches didn't they? This was how people died she thought as she continued to drive feeling the tires loosing traction. Yes, they died sliding into telephone poles after a nice day of shopping. Annette started crying. Windshield wipers batted away heavy flakes as her gloved hands rubbed off falling tears. She returned both of her hands to the steering wheel. She steered rigidly with her frightened grip.

Annette pulled up in front of her house. The trip from the mall that usually took twenty minutes had taken her an hour. She went inside and didn't even take off her wet cold shoes. Instead she closed the door and sat in the small space available in the foyer. She began to cry. Her crying turned to deep sobbing with her body heaving which caused her to knock stacks of magazines and shoe boxes to the floor. She let them lay there. She pushed the boxes to one side and lay down on top of the fallen periodicals. Annette folded her hands on her chest and looked at the ceiling, the open clear ceiling. She calmed herself and lay there quietly for perhaps an hour until finally she said, "Cocoa."

Annette walked sideways into the kitchen. With her right arm she swooped all of the unopened packages of cereal on a counter space off onto the unopened packages of napkins and paper plates piled on the kitchen floor. She maneuvered around piled boxes of unopened dishes, pans and kitchen utensils and towels next to those so that she could open an upper cupboard and pull out an unopened packet of Dutch cocoa.

She read the back, "Just add water."

Opening another cupboard she reached past multiple cans of soup and boxed juices and found a bright yellow cup. Annette moved to the sink and tore the packet of cocoa open, emptying the brown powder into the waiting yellow vessel. She added water, stirring it with her finger. Leaving the filled cup temporarily in the sink she pushed numerous clear and brown plastic bottles of multiple vitamins from in front of the microwave. Retrieving the cup from the sink she heated it up for a couple minutes and opened the microwave door. The yummy chocolate smell filled her kitchen.

"Marshmallows?" she said and looked around. "Oh forget it."

Un-Annette-like she walked in her wet shoes back to the front foyer, drinking her delicious warm cocoa.

"I will start with you," she said to the stacked paper bags with sexy ropey handles. "Yes you."

Annette alternately took drinks of her cocoa and took the shopping bags down from the pile, opening the bags and lining them up in the small open space that remained near the front door. Then she began filling the bags with varieties of items, mixing in kitchen things, sweaters, and hairspray and beach towels. She put in plastic bottles of fragranced body soap and socks. She put in baby toys she had purchased for the relatives that had remained unseen for ten years. She filled the bags and organized. Finally around three in the morning, Annette walked sidewise down her hall and went naked into her bed.

When she awoke she dressed and filled her car with the bags. Annette drove down Lark Street and stopped at Elena's house. She knocked on the door but no one answered. She unloaded the car. She left all the bags on the porch. Annette returned home and repeated her actions. During the process she unearthed a radio and turned on a rock music channel alternately playing hard rock and holiday tunes. *Weird*, she thought.

All day she loaded bags and boxes into her car. She drove back down to Lark Lane and unloaded her parcels onto other porches. Some people looked out windows at her but she figured most people were probably at work.

Mid-day she called her sister. "I'll come up after the holidays. I'll take you to lunch."

"Annette is that you?" asked Tammy.

"See you in January sis," said Annette hanging up.

She continued for days eating take-out pizzas and emptying her house.

"I wonder if I'm losing weight?" she asked herself. "My house is certainly losing weight," she laughed.

Her shoulders felt lighter. Her movements became more fluid. Her face began to take on a less tense appearance. Once after carrying two large bags up to a porch her arms lifted from her sides. They rose like two wings.

All the porches on Lark Street had received things. *What now she wondered?* Annette filled her car and drove downtown and parked near the plaza.

"Hey you. Excuse me. Come here," Annette, said to someone holding a '**Please Help**' sign.

"Take this. And here's another one," said Annette handing the woman two filled bags.

"Did your steal these?" asked the woman.

Annette laughed, "No. They stole me. Hey do you have friends? Tell them I'll be back in about half an hour."

"Thank you. " said the woman. "I'll get my friends."

"Good. I'll be back shortly. I just need to reload."

Annette's feet felt lighter. She did a little dance step and got back in her car

Annette felt like she was floating. She drove home and opened her front door and then she did something she hadn't done in years. She ran around her house. She ran and jumped on the bed and the now uncovered couch. She ran full front body forward down the hallway and then leapt into the foyer laughing and laughing. It was easier to breathe. She started loading her car with bags and boxes again. She was happy and light-headed. It was easier to lift her feet. Her stride felt wider and smoother. There was no weight on her shoulders, no ache in her back. She drove back to the plaza. A line of people was waiting for her. She parked her car and opened her trunk and car doors.

"Take whatever you want and please share what you don't want or can't use with others."

Annette smiled watching the others excited to find the sweaters and warm hats in the bags. She stepped back and then up, up into the air, first a few inches, then a few feet. Then floating above the car she let her body take her up, up and above the buildings, the trees and far, far into the sky way above the clouds.

# Twelve Shades of Green and Red

*By Jennifer U. Egan*

They were moving into Andrew's season, no doubt about it. It wasn't an accident that each of their three children had September birthdays. Yep, this was his amp up time. Elizabeth had come to enjoy it, the anticipation, the 12 days of wild crazy coupling. During three of these sexual seasons they had conceived. First Annie, their six year old daughter, second Benjamin now four, and then Nicholas just two years old and such a hilarious little one he was. Elizabeth had decided that she'd like one or two more children so she had prepared for another December conception.

The first year had shocked Elizabeth. After all they'd met at a young singles group at their church. He was an accountant and she had worked at a bank. Their courtship had moved pretty slowly at first, sweet thoughtful dates. Andrew brought her flowers sometimes and paid attention to what kind of movies she liked, (comedies) and which restaurants she preferred (Indian or Thai were her favorites). He was affectionate until December and then a different man swooped into her life, not a different person really but a very different Andrew. They became sexual and she found him to be off the charts passionate.

He was gentle with her in early December, a thoughtful lover, making her want more. But during the twelve days before Christmas, starting December 13th to be exact, he became a madman ready to pull her to bed as soon as he arrived at her apartment and she want to be pulled. Elizabeth felt he could have devoured her with his kisses and caresses. His embraces thrilled her. He explored the landscape of her body and she became a fellow adventurer with him. It had been hard to focus at work; images of his skin and nether part, erect and ready to enter would fill her mind. Sometimes she would blush from her thoughts.

"Are you alright miss?" an older man had asked her at her teller window.

"Ah, yes, just too hot, definitely too hot," she'd smiled temporarily working to push away thoughts of the happily anticipated evening ahead.

Elizabeth was relieved that she had fallen in love with Andrew before the all consuming sexual rush because had she known that antibiotics could neutralize the birth control she was using she would've added the use of a diaphragm or some other prophylactic, not condoms though. (She wanted the touch of his skin directly, all of it.) But then, Annie wouldn't have arrived nine months later. And she couldn't imagine life without the daughter she adored.

Andrew had proposed in bed, on Christmas Eve. Elizabeth didn't realize she was pregnant until January. By then everyone knew they were engaged. That Christmas eve they had managed to get dressed and leave their sexual stupor to go to the candlelight service at their church where they glowingly told their friends of their engagement. They told Elizabeth's parents on Christmas morning and shared the news with Andrew's family later Christmas day at dinner.

But back to Andrew, her dear December sexy Andrew, for various reasons this god of passion only visited during the holiday season. Oh they had sex, probably more akin to what normal couples experienced on a pretty regular basis, less so recently of course with the demands of three young children. After December 25th her boiling man would slow to a simmer but always to return without fail each year. During the twelve days before Christmas, she shared her bed with a sexual goliath, a porn star, an amorous man for whom she imagined there was no match, (or if there was Elizabeth wasn't sure she could've handled more than the man she had.)

On occasion they had talked about why this transformation occurred in December. Elizabeth's theory was that it was tied into his childhood somehow. Andrew would talk with enthusiastic descriptions about the soft sensuous feel of the stuffed animals he had received at Christmas as a little boy. He always mentioned the smells and tastes of the season in great detail, pine, cinnamon, vanilla, and nutmeg. He told her of hugs from his relations and how he loved to cuddle up with cousins and other family members as they all sat by a blazing fire in the hearth and talked together in candle light lit rooms with shadows dancing on the walls, a Christmas tree in the background. Of the childhood memories he shared with her the ones of Christmas were always the most intimate and sensuous. In response to these detailed memories, Elizabeth in gleeful anticipation of another orgy (love fest) with her amorous partner, spent time and thought on how to excite Andrew and how to feed the fire of Andrew's loins. Ah yes this was a time she looked forward to each year.

Elizabeth had found that the best scent to use in bed was cinnamon or vanilla. The second Christmas season she had learned to bake homemade cinnamon rolls and had topped them with gooey white icing. After their initial couplings she brought the warm rolls to their bed (luckily Annie was a terrific sleeper even as a baby), and they had fed the rolls to each other and licked the dripping icing from each other's skin. That had led to more *rolling* around for the two of them, which included flattening the remaining bread and making a hell of a mess, which they laughed about later. Elizabeth had learned to invest in extra lovely sheets for their king-sized bed and it was pretty much daily that they changed them together, messed them up with sweat and tangled them with their creative bonding.

Elizabeth had sought out vanilla scented candles and lotion. She actually found pine scented sheets, and cinnamon shampoo. With the computer she had explored the offerings of various lingerie sites and costume get ups. One particular success had been the year she had found the Elf see-through shimmering green nightie complete with candy cane collar, buttons and cuffs. She had added green stiletto heels and voila Benjamin had been born nine months later. Elizabeth smiled remembering. She had of course used some of the standard women's magazine suggestions; wrapping herself up like a gift, placing temporary holiday themed tattoos around her breasts and on her buttocks (much harder to put on then one would think). She had used the glitter lotions and once she had dressed up as a skanky nurse and pretended that Andrew had come to the emergency room after a sledding accident and she needed to make sure that he was okay, that everything still worked, which it did in fine fashion. No, creativity was not missing and this year she had found something that she thought would delight and inspire him even more, which was great as she wanted them to conceive again this year.

After Ben was born she had asked both her in-laws and her own parents to take the children overnight sometimes during the holiday season after December 13th. Elizabeth told them that this allowed Andrew and her to better prepare the holidays for their children. The first couple of years their parents had happily taken their grandchildren for overnights. This allowed Andrew and Elizabeth greater time and freedom for their lovemaking but after Nicholas, (who usually woke up at night) was born, they offered far less frequently. Their parents were older and didn't do well without a good night's sleep. This reduced Andrew and Elizabeth's intense love making time. They loved each other and they loved their children. They would just have to make the most of the time they had.

On December thirteenth Andrew began his transformation. The kids were put to bed and Elizabeth lit candles around the bedroom. They were off to a slow but passionate start but let's face it life's demands of work and children were causing a leak in the well so to speak.

By December 18<sup>th</sup>, Elizabeth donned her special outfit. She requested that Andrew wait nude in their bed with the lights out. Elizabeth prepared herself in the bathroom. She had found a new site for stimulating outfits. Hot red heels pulled on she flung open their bathroom door to the awe of Andrew. There stood his wife of seven years in a mini see through flaming red nightie with alternating flashing boob lights and a crotch light that glowed green. It was the only signal he needed. Flesh pummeled flesh as their enthusiastic lovemaking ensued, once with a brief rest followed by a rush of back and neck kisses with a repeat performance. Lights still flashing and welcoming they were beginning their third round when Nicholas's scream pierced their sexual fog.

"MOMMY!"

On automatic Elizabeth ran from their room and down the hall. Nicholas was crying in his bed. She picked him up and hugged him to her.

"You're okay honey. Mommy is here. Shh. Shh."

She rocked him and he calmed. Elizabeth heard the toilet flush down the hall and realized it was probably Annie. It was then Elizabeth realized her body was still glowing with battery-operated lights.

"Here Nicholas, mommy will lie down with you until you go to sleep." She quickly settled him under his covers and climbed in with him under the sheets and comforter.

"Mommy?" It was Elizabeth in the doorway. "Mommy I can't sleep. Can I get in bed with you and Nicholas?"

"Sure, umm, Annie I was just going to go back to my bed."
She was trying to find the buttons to turn off the flashing lights.
There was one in the panties and one for each cup of the bra. She
found the one near the crotch. *Thank goodness she thought to
herself.* She located one breast button and pushed it. Only one breast
was flashing when Annie climbed in with them. Nicholas had fallen
back asleep.

"Mommy what's that?" asked Annie.

"What's what Annie?"

"The light mommy?" Elizabeth's body became rigid. She
removed her hand from Nicholas's shoulder and placed her palm
firmly over her flashing left tit. Where was that off button?

"Oh they are special holiday pajamas."

"Can I get some? We'll have pajama day in school after
vacation."

"Ah, maybe. There are lots of secrets at this time of year."

"Oh I hope I get some, maybe with light up slippers too."

"Light up slippers? Good idea."

"Good night mommy. Oh mommy I love Benjamin and
Nicholas but I think I want a sister. "

There was a pause then Elizabeth said, "I'm working on it
Annie, believe me I am."

"I know mommy. I know you are."

# Snowball

*By Jennifer U. Egan*

Gutter completely cleaned, lawn manicured, house touched up with paint. Hands down, Ed's was the best-kept house and yard on the street. True he was retired and possibly had more time than some of his neighbors but he worked hard and kept up his part of the block. When he took his daily walk exactly three times around the block each day, it pained him to see high grass shooting up on the sides of driveways and unweeded side gardens. There was no way around it these neighbors were simply slovenly. Why, they should be forced to move to apartments rather than have the privilege of having a yard. Oh, he had seen plenty of poorly tended yards in his day. Horrific images of places he'd delivered the mail to popped up in his mind periodically. Once in a while thoughts like this kept him awake at night. The counselor he had gone to for that one appointment had given him a great idea, which he had used on numerous occasions.

"When those ideas pop up Ed, why don't you just picture yourself with a lawnmower or trimmer and cut them down. Hey, it's a dream right? So you can do it pretty damn quick, don't you think?"

This had comforted Ed and he had lost very little sleep ever since.

Recently he had noticed neighbors putting up those messy Halloween decorations. This week some of the white spider web material had blown over into his yard. He had not complained. He had just raked it up along with the leaves but this was a new low. The people next door really should be more considerate. He opened a beer and turned on the news.

"An extremely early snowfall is expected this year beginning tomorrow evening."

Oh good, he thought. Snow would cover all the imperfections of his block, the unweeded gardens, and unraked leaves. He loved the snow and as always he would have the first and best shoveled front porch and walkway. He welcomed snow and he was ready.

For once the weather person was precisely correct. Ed woke to find an inch and a half of snow covering everything. Even before having his Raisin Bran he got dressed and headed to his garage for the snow shovel. He got to it and then walked around the block once.

Yep, he had been the very first to get that job done. He returned to his house and opened his living room drapes and watched his neighbors heading to their cars without shoveling anything. "Lazy bastards," he mumbled as milk and bran slid out of his mouth and down his chin.

When Ed woke up the next morning, he looked out his window first thing. No new snow. He ate breakfast and got dressed. Time to take his daily three around the block. He opened his front door and there smack in the middle of his porch was one snowball. Some kid had probably thrown it in the other yard and it had landed here by accident. Then he noticed a small silver glint extending from its left side. At first he thought it was a piece of metal. Ed leaned down and picked up the hard packed ball, more like ice really, and picked around what turned out to be a piece of silver paper. It was all folded up. When he opened it a burst of peppermint accosted his nostrils. He could see that it was a piece of foil that had been wrapped around gum. On the white side that would have embraced the gum was one printed word written in permanent marker, "HA!"

"Weird," he said out loud. He went inside and threw the paper in the kitchen trash. Then he got his snow shovel and made sure he removed all of the particles of the snowball from his porch. He got the outside broom and finished the job. "Weird," he said again.

The rest of the day he took his walk, read the paper, cleaned up the kitchen and ate a can of soup while he watched the news and weather. More snow was expected.

The next morning he looked out to find a soft dusting of snow had fallen. He ate his Raisin Bran and went to get his shovel. But when he opened his front door not only did he find a new thin layer of snow he also found a neat row of five snowballs each with a piece of silver sticking out from their top. Ed set his shovel aside and stepped on one of the snowballs, smashing it with one hefty footfall right there on his porch. He picked up the silver paper, opened it and again the word "Ha!" was written clearly on the paper.

Ed looked at the other four snowballs.

"You're all giving me the finger, that's what you're doing," he yelled at the cold white orbs. Ed first looked around to make sure no one in the neighborhood was watching him and then he stomped forcefully on the four balls. Each one released another ominous silver piece of paper which when opened revealed another hearty laugh at him. "Ha!"

Ed stuffed all of the papers into his coat pocket and proceeded to shovel and then sweep off his messy porch. He didn't feel like taking a walk. Ed tried to clean his kitchen and read the newspaper but thoughts of the snowballs and silver papers kept jumping into mind. The mental lawn mower tool wasn't useful in getting rid of these.

When the weatherman predicted more snow that night. Ed felt his heart begin to race. He decided to close the living room drapes and peek out the slit between them. Yes that's what he would do. He would watch and discover who the gum-chewing bastard was.

Ed always went to bed by 9:30 pm but that night he sat very focused and quiet by the window. He saw children making a snowman across the street. Some were throwing snowballs. Other kids were running in front of his house. He watched neighbors arrive home. One seemed to be chewing gum, a woman, but he wasn't completely sure. By half past midnight, he drifted off to sleep. He woke at six in the morning, disoriented at first. Where was he? His shoulder ached and he felt stiff but he jumped out of his overstuffed chair and raced to the door. He turned on the porch light. Now there was one long row of snowballs three snowballs high completely across his porch each with a silver glint showing from its exterior.

"WHO THE HELL CHEWS THAT MUCH GUM?"

Ed stomped on the wall of snowballs and collected all of the pieces of paper. Most had the word, "Ha!" written on them but some had the words, "Ha, ha" and even "Ha, ha, ha" with a smile drawn on them. Things were escalating.

One of Ed's neighbors was heading out to his car to go to work.

"Hi, Ed," he called.

—

43

Ed froze. He looked at the neighbor. Was he chewing gum?

"It's not funny," he called at his neighbor.

The neighbor looked at him oddly and then got in his car glancing at Ed again as he drove away.

Ed went in and called the police, "I am calling to report an act of terrorism."

"Yes sir. Tell me what is going on and where."

"It's on my front porch. Someone or a group is leaving more and more snowballs with cruel messages."

The lady on the other end of the line was quiet and then, "Sir it is illegal to make prank calls to the police department. We are far too busy to have to deal with jokesters. I am noting your number now. Do not do this again."

Ed heard the dial tone. She had hung up.

Ed didn't want to go for a walk. He didn't want to eat. He needed to plan. He stood leaning against his kitchen counter for a long time.

"That's it. Oh yeah. I'll show them."

Ed brought his shovel and broom and placed them inside by the door but he kept the door closed and he did not clean off the messy front porch.

"This will shock them," he said out loud smiling, "Oh yeah. They will be oh so surprised."

He laughed and was hungry now. He actually cooked himself an egg and didn't even clean the pan out. Oh yeah. He could do this.

He watched the news and the weather report only to learn more snow was expected.

"Bring it on," Ed said smugly sitting comfortably in his overstuffed chair, which he had moved back in front of the television.

Ed went to bed at his regular time, 9:30. He slept well and in the morning he looked out of his upstairs bedroom window. Yep, there was about two inches of new snow. He ate his Raisin Bran and then got dressed warmly, ready to take a three time around the block stroll. He opened his front door and there completely blocking his doorway was a wall of perfect snowballs, layer upon layer, far too many to even bother counting, each individual ball with a silver taunting piece of paper protruding from its snow hold.

At first frozen in place, Ed stood in shocked silence staring at the wall. The fucking mocking wall blocking his way, polluting his porch, defiling his perfect house and yard. Then with his ungloved hands he started punching at the frozen balls creating some holes in this blockage. His skin tore and blood flashed on the pure whiteness. He punched and kicked in a frenzy until he fell through the wall onto his porch where he continued to hit the wall with his bloody hands and his booted feet such that crusty snow and his bodily fluids were flying into his front door, into the hallway and the kitchen.

A strong cramp seized his chest. First he knelt and then fell flattened on his front porch, snow melting under him, a silver piece of paper flapping between the clenched fingers of his left hand.

# THE OPEN HOUSE
By *G.Z. Hill*

Marvin stomped down the sidewalk three paces ahead of Claire. It was so like him to walk fast, even when his walking fast days were over. She pulled on his overcoat and tugged him back, slowing the clicking of his cane, forcing him to turn. Forcing him to wait for her.

"This isn't going to kill you," she smiled.

"Might."

Claire rolled her eyes, "They're nice people."

"He thinks he's better than us."

"No he doesn't, he just wears suits."

"Never waves."

Claire looped her arm through the sleeve of his long tweed overcoat, to slow him down. "Isn't it pretty out tonight?" She pointed to the blue lights hanging off the Morgan's eaves as they passed.

"Garish," he mumbled.

"Oh look Marv, it's starting to snow."

He pulled his hat lower and hunched his shoulders. "Hope it stops."

---

"I love snow at Christmas." She lifted her face up to the falling flakes and watched them swirl overhead, dusting her face.

"Snow is nothing but work."

"Well, it's pretty and you don't have to go out in it."

"Like hell. I have to shovel the damn stuff."

"The kids can come over and do it."

"What kids?"

Claire adjusted the red bowed package on the large Santa tin she carried. "They would come over and help if we asked them. If they thought we needed their help, all we have to do is call."

"Don't need them." He muttered.

Claire took a deep breath as they crossed the street and headed down the next block. She had been looking forward to the open house all week. She smiled at him, "I want you to behave tonight."

"Not stayin' more than ten minutes."

Claire tugged at his sleeve forcing him to turn around. "We have been invited to the open house and we will stay longer than ten minutes."

"Nope. I'm going after the hellos. There's a game at eight, I plan to watch."

"You have taped it."

"Not the same."

"Well, we're not rushing out so you can watch a basketball game that you already have on the DVR."

"Wait and see."

"And leave me there by myself?"

"You'll have a house full of people to talk to. I won't be missed."

"Marvin."

He heaved a sigh and turned and looked at her. He could tell by the set of her mouth that she was getting angry.

She said, "You're not going to leave me and walk home alone."

"Might. Wait and see."

Claire took a deep breath, fighting for patience as she followed along next to him, watching as he took halting steps as the sidewalk was starting to disappear under a thin layer of snow.

She said, after a moment, "Thank you for agreeing to come tonight."

"I'm doing this because I don't want you walking three blocks in the damn dark, but I'm not staying. That Henderson fella will be there and after five minutes he'll start talking about the Bible and ask if we want to go to Church with him tomorrow."

"And like every year since we've lived here, he's asked and you've said no."

He nodded, stomping through the dusting of snow. "I don't like his church."

"You've never been to his church."

"Don't plan to either."

Claire looked down the block and saw Wagner's house lit up with a strings of white lights covering all their shrubs and looped through the branches along the bottom half of the old maple that stood on their front lawn. Through the front bay window she could see people talking and clustering around the piano. She knew that Marvin would have a fit if he were asked to sing along.

Marvin stood dumbfounded as he looked past the lights towards the nodding mechanical reindeer that sat under some trees along the side of the house. All along the fence line were hundreds of red and green lights twinkling. "I sure as hell wouldn't want to pay their damn light bill."

Claire tugged his sleeve and shook her head. Realizing, like always, Marvin would find something negative to say about everything. She wasn't going to let him spoil her evening. Not this time, not like last year. She missed having friends over for dinner or a card game, but as Marvin had said many times . . .*people stay too damn long and don't know when the hell to go home*!

Marvin stopped as they reached the front gate. "Can you hear that?"

"What?"

"That damn dog is barking."

"Don't worry about the dog."

"I don't like dogs and you know it." He glared down at her. "I want to go back home."

"No. We're already here, we're going to go inside and have a good time." She pulled him down, tilted up and brushed his clean-shaven cheek with a kiss.

"What was that for?" He growled.

Claire pointed up into the hanging branch over the gate. "Mistletoe." For a second she thought she caught the hint of a smile, but it disappeared back into the scowl he seemed to wear all the time. The flash of the smile, reminded her or when he was younger and laughed all the time.

When they got close to the front door, Marvin stopped walking. "I hate dogs."

"Keep your cane away from him and you'll be fine."

"It's a damn yapper. Yap yap yap yap. Damn thing yaps all the time. I can hear it all the way to our house."

"I doubt it. We're three blocks away."

"Just sayn'." He looked down at the tin she was holding. "Probably didn't think to leave some of those at home."

Claire smiled as she hit the doorbell. "We have a whole tin full at home."

"Good!" Marvin adjusted the wool scarf at his neck. "Don't tell them they're loaded with rum. That will teach the churchy bastards."

Claire turned him to face her. "I want to see you smile."

"Don't feel like it."

The door was thrown open wide as Peggy waved them inside with quick hugs. "Oh I'm so happy you made it, we're just gathering around the piano. Here, let me take your coats."

Marvin allowed her to take his hat and scarf but he took his time taking off his coat. He watched as Claire unbuttoned her long blue coat, then she turned and flashed him a wink.

---

Claire handed over the tin. "Just a little something for you to enjoy later."

Down the hall a small terrier bolted right up to Marvin's leg, circling and barking.

Claire saw that Marvin was starting to lift his cane, so she gently reached over and held it firm, then she crouched down and patted the dogs head. He stopped barking and began to lick her hand, wagging his tail as fast as it would go.

"What a sweetie." Claire stood and watched as the dog turned and began barking again at Marvin. She leaned into Marvin and whispered, "Ignore him, he'll warm up to you." She pulled him down the hall into the living room where there were several neighbors waiting. A few people she didn't know smiled and other's came over and gave warm hugs. Everyone watched as Marvin shuffled and swung his cane from side to side as the dog barked next to his leg darting in front and then dashing behind him, then back to his side, all the time barking louder and louder trying to keep away from the swinging cane.

Peggy rushed towards them, "Do you want me to put Skipper out?"

"Oh no, he's fine." Claire said, then smiled as she nudged Marvin towards the dining room table where food and drinks and been set up. There was a side table with cold drinks and a big punch bowl next to a coffee urn. On the dining table were assorted platters of cold cuts, cookies and small sandwiches, all piled and displayed on large Christmas plates.

"Here, eat something." Claire led him to the table and handed him a small plate.

"Where's the real food?" He grumbled.

"These are just snacks. Take something."

He leaned down and plucked a stuffed mushroom off a platter and stuffed it in his mouth as he looked around. He whispered next to her, "Where the hell are the men?"

Peggy watched Marvin and then over hearing, she said to Marvin. "The men are down the hall. There's some kind of a game they wanted to see." She smiled at Claire, "I think we girls are going to be left alone for a while. Come on Marvin, I'll show you the way."

Marvin followed along ignoring the barking dog that was right at his heels.

Claire worried as she watched Marvin walk down the hell towards the family room. She knew he wouldn't last very long, once she was out of his sight. She watched as he glanced over his shoulder and gave a wide swing of his cane at the barking dog. She thought about following, but then decided maybe he would do okay.

No point in causing a scene

............................................

Marvin frowned as he followed Peggy to the back of the house where men were sitting in rows of tubby reclining chairs facing the wall sized TV screen.

Everyone looked up as he came into the room. Several men stood and smiled. Peggy's husband dashed over, on his head was a red Santa hat, where the snowball on the peak bobbed as he greeted Marvin with a handshake. He made fast introductions around the room and then motioned Marvin towards the front row where an empty chair and large ottoman faced the wall-to-wall TV screen.

Marvin grumbled as he tapped his cane across the floor and sat heavily into the leather chair. He settled back and took the cup of hot cider one of the men had poured for him.

He looked up at the screen remembering years ago when he used to go to the old Royal Cinema's in his neighborhood. He didn't like the movies they made today, too much noise, too many people sitting close and talking, too damn much sex. He wished they made some good old westerns like they used to. Those were the good old days.

Marvin leaned his head back on the headrest so he could see the whole screen. He squinted. The screen was huge. He knew for sure he'd get a blinding bitch of a headache sitting so damn close and wondered why in the hell they had stuck him in the front row.

Taking a sip from the cup, he tried to hear what the men were talking about. With his bad left ear, he figured he would just ignore them. He didn't want to come anyway and with any luck he wouldn't have to stay very long. He glanced around and realized that no one was paying any attention to him so he looked up at the screen he saw that the game was about to start. He stared down at the dog that was hunched at his feet, ready to leap.

Just as Marvin lifted his legs to the ottoman, the dog landed on his lap. Staring at him with dark moist eyes a moment, the dog turned, circled and wiggled next to him and with a sigh, laid his head on Marvin's leg.

Marvin dropped his hand down on the back of the dog to push him off and instead the dog licked his hand. *Damn dog*, he muttered. He looked at the fluff of fur with soft eyes. He figured he could probably tolerate the dog a few minutes, since he had stopped barking. He watched the dog close his eyes and give off a soft sigh.

Marvin looked out the window and could see that snow was falling hard. Down the hall he could hear Claire's voice above the others as they sang Jingle Bells. He shook his head in disgust. They must be singing pretty loud for him to hear them, he just hoped to hell their damn singing wouldn't drown out the game.

He looked around the room. He might not like these people, had no use for most of them but with a lot of Christmas memories, over the years, he decided that maybe this one wouldn't be worst Christmas he'd ever had, now that the game was ready to start.

He sipped his cider and tasted cinnamon, then sipped again. *Well I'll be dammed!* He smiled.

His hand dropped down to the dog's head.

Sure enough. He sipped again to be sure. . .

Yep! He tasted a bite of Whiskey.

He glanced over and gave a nod to Santa hat, who was smiling across the room.

He hated to admit it . . . but. . .maybe Santa hat wasn't so bad after all.

The game was just about to start. Marvin took a fast glance across the room to the window. Snow was now coming down so thick that all he could see were flakes taking away the night.

Maybe a little snow outside would make Claire happy. She thought it was pretty. He didn't. Just watching the fat flakes piling up outside made him frown. He just hoped to hell he wouldn't fall on his ass going home. He could just see Claire now, all in a dither, as he lay sprawled on the sidewalk with a broken hip. If that happened then he could just blame her. Tell her that they shouldn't have come. That they should have stayed home like had wanted. That would show her!

But until then . . .he looked at Santa hat and tipped his empty cup. He figured he had time for one more drink, maybe even another one after that as long as Claire didn't know.

He decided not to worry about the snow.

"Merry Christmas Marvin." Santa hat handed him a fresh drink. "Do you want me to take Skipper off your lap?"

Marvin looked down at the dog and scowled. "He ain't bothern' me none."

The room went quiet as one of the men lowered the lights and the volume was cranked up.

Looking towards the door, he saw Claire waving her arms smiling, trying to get his attention. He waved her away and focused on the screen. What with the snow coming down hard and the game starting, he figured they might as well wait until half time. No point in rushing back home now.

He sipped his drink, letting his other hand fall down on the dog's soft head.

Closing his eyes against the glare off the giant screen, he leaned his head back and listened to the game. Taking one last sip from his drink he hoped to hell he didn't fall asleep and start snoring.

But if he did. If that happened. Then what the hell did they expect, inviting a ninety-five year old man out so late, then turning off the lights.

Marvin figured he earned the right to do as he pleases. He could sleep not sleep, snore, and have another drink if he felt like it. He opened his eyes a crack and looked around the room. No one was paying any attention to him. He looked over at the door and saw that Claire had gone back to the living room.

He smiled, satisfied the he would be left alone. He closed his eyes again and rested. If Claire asked, he would tell her he had a good enough time. Tell her he was glad it had started snowing, because he knew she liked to have snow at Christmas. If she insisted that someone drive them home, he wouldn't complain.

He knew that sometimes he was stubborn and maybe this next year he would try to smile more. Maybe even have Peggy and Santa hat over for a drink. Claire would like that.

Marvin didn't make a sound when he had the heart attack, he didn't hear the buzzer. Didn't know that the men hadn't noticed that he was gone until they turned on the lights at half time.

Truth be known.

Marvin had been enjoying himself.

They found him looking peaceful, his eyes closed. Skipper had rested his head on Marvin's hand and watched over him until Claire could be called in from the other room.

# Hat

*By Jennifer U. Egan*

Jack's mother always wore a holiday hat or headband. One year she had insisted that they all wear light-up reindeer antlers to the downtown parade. But as they moved into the teen years, he and his sister would conveniently leave the head gear in the car or verbally refuse.

"There is no way! What if my friends see me?"

So Grace had been left to carry on the tradition on her own and now even though Jack and Susan were adults she continued the ritual. All evening out of the corner of his eye Grace's hat had drawn his attention. When she laughed this year's pink sequined Santa hat had tilted. Jack found himself zoning out from the dinner conversation and watching it.

This one didn't even have blinking lights or a bell.

"MOM!"

Everyone stopped and looked at Jack.

"What Jack? What's the matter?"

"Your hat moved!"

Grace raised her wine glass to him, "A little too much holiday cheer?"

But then something from inside the hat bumped out the cloth again.

Jack got up from his chair.

His mother screamed and ran to the bathroom with Jack in hot pursuit. Grace locked herself in.

"Mom! What's in there?"

"You're crazy," she yelled through the closed door, "Go back to the table."

There was a pause and then she heard footsteps moving back towards the dining room.

Grace tipped the hat off her head and pulled the small mouse out by his tail, "Nice work sweetie."

She opened the cabinet under the sink and placed the rodent inside careful to close it in silently. She looked in the mirror.

"Oh that won't do."

Grace grabbed a comb and raked the small turds from the top of her hair into the sink. She turned on the faucet. A few went down and a couple didn't. No matter she thought. She set the hat back on her head.

"Gotcha Jack," she smiled.

Grace opened the bathroom door and walked back to the table.

# Puppet

*By Jennifer U. Egan*

"Nick, will you wait here with Daniel for just a couple minutes while I get some vitamins. It's my last errand, promise."

"Okay Jessie but then let's hit the road. I've got to get up early for work tomorrow."

Nick had their three month old fast asleep in a front pack and took Daniel's hand. "Mommy has one more thing to do. Let's go over and look at the toys okay?"

"Okay."

They walked over to one of the kiosks set up in the mall during the holidays. This one had colorful stuffed animals all over it.

Daniel let go of his dad's hand and went to something fluffy and very green. He started talking to it. When Jessie came out of the vitamin store carrying a small bag Daniel was still in deep conversation with what turned out to be a frog puppet.

"Jessie, come here." Nick pulled her aside. "Daniel has been talking to this puppet and making it talk pretty much non-stop for about fifteen minutes."

"Fifteen minutes? That is wonderful. What has he been saying?"

"God I don't know. But he's talking. Isn't that what you've been worried about?"

Jessica knelt down near Daniel. "Hey who is your friend?"

"This is Froggy mommy. He doesn't want to live in the mall anymore."

"He's kind of tired of that huh? Does he plan on moving to a pond somewhere?"

"I don't know," Daniel looked puzzled.

"Do you want to try him out? He's actually a puppet," said the man behind the counter of the kiosk.

"Sure. That would be great," said Jessica.

The grey haired older man came out with a key and unlocked a cable that had been locking the frog puppet to the counter.

*They must have trouble with shoplifting* Jessica thought.

The man handed the large yellow and black-eyed frog to Jessica. Two long arms and legs dangled from the puppet's sides as Jessica found the mouth opening in the back of the frog's head.

"Hey Daniel," Jessica had the frog say. "I think I would like to be near a pond. I could see my frog friends that way. Do you want to hear my frog croak?"

Daniel smiled and Jessica had the frog open his mouth wide and make two large rivet sounds.

"It's a hugging puppet," offered the salesman.

"Oh that's cool." She took her hand from the mouth and put them both in the frog's arms. "Want a hug Daniel?"

Daniel leaned in for a hug and Jessica via the puppet gave him a big hug back.

Smiling, Nick was standing nearby and rocking Ella, now sound asleep.

Jessica turned and mouthed the words. *"Oh, my God* and BUY THIS!"

Nick nodded his head, "Daniel, say goodbye to the frog. We have to get home."

Daniel hugged the puppet hard crushing Jessica's hand that was still inside. She winced but then said, "Bye Daniel. Nice to meet you."

"Bye Froggy. I love you."

Jessica handed the puppet back to the kind man.

"Time to go."

They all walked down the center of the mall towards the exit doors to the parking lot. Daniel kept looking behind him at the stuffed animal kiosk. Nick and Jessica were smiling at each other.

"Go buy it!" Jessica mouthed again.

"Wait. Make it a surprise!" whispered Nick.

"There is only one!" Jessica whispered.

"What mommy?"

"I said what fun! I have macaroni at home for dinner tonight. Your favorite right?'

"Do frogs like macaroni and cheese mommy?"

"I don't know."

They fastened the kids in their car seats and started the car up. It was cold and the car always took a while to heat up. Daniel had his winter coat zipped up and they had tucked an extra blanket around Ella.

It took a half hour to get home. Jessica put Ella in her crib and went back to the kitchen to fix dinner. She had the baby monitor on so that she would hear Ella when she woke up. Daniel was building with duplos quietly in the living room. Nick walked into the kitchen.

"Nick. Go back and get the Frog!"

"Tonight? Jessie, it's cold I'm hungry. It can wait until tomorrow."

"Nick, we briefly got our little chatterbox back. Ever since Ella's birth he has turned into this quiet little mouse. Go get that Frog."

"Really Jessie? You want me to drive all the way back to the mall tonight?"

"Nick, oh I'm sorry. But yes, yes I do. The frog may already be gone. Gone! Then what? We've had three months of quiet kid. Let's help him get back to his usual self."

"Do you want to go?"

"Yes, and if I could hand over my breasts to you I would!"

"Hmmmm. Father abuse."

Jessica smiled, "We signed up for this."

"I'll make you a deal."

"I'm listening."

"Waffles on Christmas morning."

"You got it. Now go before Froggy is gone forever. Hurry."

Nick started to put his coat back on. "Well bye Jessie and Daniel. I have to go back to school for a meeting and then I'll be home. Daniel, promise me you won't eat all the macaroni and cheese."

"I won't daddy."

Nick was out the door.

By eight o'clock Daniel had had his bath and story and was sound asleep. Jessica was nursing Ella in the living room rocking chair and starting to worry. Then the door opened and in popped a green head.

"Is this my new home?"

"Oh this is so great! Hide it Nick. Oh he will love this," and she hugged Nick gently with the baby between them.


On Christmas morning they sat in pajamas and Nick started to hand out presents one at a time. The first he handed to Daniel. Daniel found Duplos from Grandma Ellen inside. He wanted to open them and play but Nick said. "Hey buddy let's keep going here."

He handed one to Jessica. She opened the highly scotch-taped package to find a beautiful yellow colander from Daddy and Daniel. Jessica hugged them both.

"Daniel would you open this one for Ella? She can't open things yet."

Daniel opened a squeaky rattle and pressed it to make the sound for Ella. Ella cooed and smiled. Nick's turn was next. He opened paper to find a new red sweater from Jessica and Daniel. He wrapped it around his neck like a scarf at first and they laughed.

"Whose that package for there?" asked Jessica.

"Oh this one? Hmmm let's see. It's for Daniel," from Santa.

Daniel jumped up and clapped his hands and ran to get the package. With one quick rip a large yellow eye with a black iris stared out at all of them. Two more tears and Froggy was out.

"Froggy! Oh Froggy!" Daniel hugged his new toy. He jumped up and down. "Oh Santa, thank you. Thank you."

Daniel ran around the room hugging Froggy. The rest of the presents could wait. His new friend had arrived.

"Oh I knew you'd come Froggy. Just like you told me you would. Oh Froggy."

"What will you name him Daniel?"

Daniel looked surprised, "It's Froggy mommy. You know that."

"Froggy it is then."

Ella began to cry a little and Jessica took her from the baby seat, carried her to the rocking chair and began to nurse her. "Nick, does this make the trip back to the mall worth it?"

"Waffles."

"Oh you and Ella are the food focused ones that's for sure. Let me feed her and you're next. I will keep my end of the bargain."

Nick smiled.

Daniel was busy carrying Froggy all around the house, giving him the tour. "This is the kitchen and mommy is going to feed us waffles. I like mine with applesauce and butter."

Daniel started up the stairway, "And now I'll show you my bedroom where we'll sleep. There is plenty of room in my bed for both of us Froggy."

Daniel was back to talking non-stop like he used to.

"Will we regret this?" asked Nick.

"Only when Ella starts to speak and they're both chattering at the same time!" laughed Jessica. She handed Ella to Nick and plugged in the waffle iron.

At breakfast they gave Froggy his own chair. They all made him talk at times but then Daniel began to tell them what Froggy wanted to say or what he was thinking.

"Does Froggy like flies or waffles better?" asked Nick.

"He loves Waffles!" and Daniel began to feed a large forkful to Froggy. A boundary had to be set.

"Daniel, Froggy is a puppet and puppets don't eat real food. Otherwise he may have to go for a ride in the washing machine and I'm not sure he'd like that."

"Oh I think he might like it!" laughed Daniel.

"Son, no real food for Froggy," said dad.

"Okay."

After breakfast they cleaned up, dressed up in warm clothing and went for a walk down to the neighborhood park. Daniel had Nick and Jessica take turns holding one of Froggy's hands while he held the other. They would run with Froggy between them. Sometimes they would twirl Froggy around and upside down and everyone laughed.

When they got to the park, Froggy got to ride on the swing. (Belly down wasn't usually allowed but they were making an exception for their new green friend.) Froggy went down the slide again and again, sometimes with Daniel and sometimes on his own. They stayed out for hours and then they went home and opened more presents. Daniel told Froggy about each one and played with the duplos with Froggy later, building him a toy duplo robot and then a little car while Nick and Jessica took turns holding Ella and preparing the turkey dinner. They skyped grandparents far away in New Jersey and smelled the house fill with the great smells of the coming Christmas dinner. Shortly before two o'clock Daniel started closing his eyes. He hugged Froggy to him and walked upstairs.

"I'll come up and read you a story in just a minute honey," Jessica called up after him.

Jessica passed off Ella to Nick. She checked on the roasting turkey, which looked like it was doing just fine. She was pleased to see that the dough for the rolls was rising well. Jessica then padded up the carpeted stairs in her socks and opened the door to Daniel's room. The frog puppet was in Daniel's little rocking chair and Daniel was sound asleep on his bed.

---

"He needed a nap," said Froggy.

"Yes he did," said Jessica.

She quietly left the room, closing the door quietly behind her and started down the stairs and then she stopped.

# First Year Gone

*By Jennifer U. Egan*

The large cat was asleep by the foot of Jane's chair, Ron's chair really. She'd never sat in it when he was alive. This had been his territory, his gentle domain.

Missing embraces, she snuggled into the cushions.

"Miss that," that she said out loud.

Louie looked up briefly and then scrunched his head back between his furry shoulders.

"You miss your buddy don't you Louie? Oh, yes."

She got up and went to the sliding glass door to the porch. Pushing the lock up she slid it open. The electrical plug was at her feet. She placed it into the outside socket. The small fir tree just beyond the dining room window came alive. Green and red lights circled the tree and reflected off the window.

"You liked this Ron, remember?"

She stood in the doorway between the outside and the inside worlds, savoring the cold catch of wind off the snow. Then too chilled, she stepped back inside and slid the door closed and locked it.

Snow was falling again.

"Nice for her great grandchildren," she thought.

It had been sweet to see them at her granddaughter's today, decorating Christmas cookies. So much colored frosting on faces and fingers. How exciting for them.

Her mind traveled back to a time when she and Ron were a young couple. They had problems with that old car. In the cold weather they'd had to open the hood of the car and adjust things so often just to get it started while their two daughters shivered in the back seat.

"Oh, that was awful," she laughed, remembering. "So many miles you and I."

And then he was there. Not completely solid but there just the same. Standing in the snow outside the window. It was her husband of twenty years ago, a stronger, healthier Ron, before the cancer, before the decline.

Standing in his overcoat, outside the window, snowflakes catching on his shoulders. He was standing there, his glasses on, looking in at her.

She gasped, putting her hand to her mouth. "Ron! Ron!" She stepped forward toward the window, one step and then another until she was just next to it feeling the cold from the glass between them.

"Oh, I miss you Ron."

He smiled and stepped forward placing his ungloved hand flat against the pane. She reached forward and flattened her hand against the window, against his.

Their gaze locked silently for one long moment.

The void returned.

Large soft flakes drifted through the space where he had been.

# PTFD

*By Jennifer U. Egan*

*Manicotti noodles ripping as she attempted to push, shove, and cajole the cheese mixture into the reluctant tubes. Peppered and highly spiced tomato sauce, bubbling and spitting, burning specks of red liquid onto her bare arms and clothing. How many tubes for how many people? How many tubes for how many?*

Delilah's eyes flew open. A small lake of sweat sat on her chest and dripped from her underarms. The digital clock light glared 2 A.M. It was the third night in a row. How many more sleepless nights awaited her?

The holidays were fun right?

Fourteen people for twelve days, ate, chewed, and swallowed. Mouths moved, talking. Fingers reached for and pushed, snacks into their open orifices. Cheese covered crackers and crunchy carrots dipped in humus lead to loud masticating noises, which stole all the silence in the room. Crumbs of morning bagels stuck under bottom lips and on chins. Mouths moved, talked, ate, drank, nonstop. And the baby walked and chewed on pillows, paper, everything.

She had watched jaws going up and down and cheeks filling, bulging and then reducing in size. She had watched rather than listened.

Beforehand there had been big trips to Costco and Food 4 less. She had frozen turkeys, a ham and bags of bagels. She had filled the refrigerator with butter, cheese, and vegetables. The old frig in the garage held the prepared manicotti, frozen and waiting in its freezer section. It had made odd rumble sounds when she approached.

"Don't you dare die, no way, not now. They are all coming and you know it."

The frig had silenced its growls and returned to its usual purr, clearly afraid of this cooker, shopper woman. After all her husband's building tools were in clear sight on the other side of the garage. Metal that could hurt, might slash through an old refrigerator door, hammers that could dent deeply.

Yes, Delilah had muscles from kneading, mixing, chopping and carrying groceries and pans filled with meals to freeze, for the masses, her family masses and his.

And the kitchen frig, she hated it. Who the hell had invented the side-by-side door refrigerator? That had been a gift. Oh yeah. She had liked the shiny white monolith until the first time she attempted to place a large sheet cake in the refrigerator section. Thank God they'd kept the dinosaur out back. The vertical two-door fridge had proved itself worthless. Nothing of any size could be placed there. Only skinny containers made their way into the narrow storage area. Worthless, worthless, crazy worthless.

With the approaching holiday season Delilah knew it was freezer time for survival. She knew that the time she prepped now would allow her visiting time with her kids later. Ah yes, less pressure, less stress, a happier holiday season.

She was glad that Andy had been out of the house the day she had the meltdown. Tearing the year-old frozen veggie bags out on the kitchen floor and ripping them apart had felt wonderful and freeing. Ah, what a mess. And when she was done raging she had started cleaning up first with the snow shovel and then with the broom.

"I see you cleaned out the freezer," was all her husband said when he went to get his nightly Popsicle.

She had only smiled and said nothing.

But now it was over. The two turkeys had been stuffed and roasted. The homemade cranberry sauce was long gone and more could've been eaten. Rolls, pasta, salad, endless meals, they had fed fourteen people for twelve days. If she were rich what would she have done? Hired a cook or taken everyone to dinner?

Lying in bed she pictured her entire clan wearing curtains over their mouths. At first she pictured them wearing black pieces of cloth draped across the lower portions of their faces like women in the middle east but since it was her imagination she changed them to all wearing different fabrics, and with a metal piece inside to extend the fabric, covering the mouth but then protruding out from it, like a cloth snout of sorts. In this image she pictured them lifting forkfuls of food underneath and up into their mouth cavities. She didn't have to watch, or hear or experience all the jaw smashing and teeth abrasion. She muted this image, ah silence.

Delilah began to laugh quietly at first. Her husband was sound asleep beside her. But then she giggled and it infected her entire body like a long domino run giggling and wiggling loudly throughout her being until she was loudly belly laughing which of course stopped the snoring and woke Andy.

"What the hell Delilah?"

"CRANBERRY SAUCE," She yelled at the ceiling.

"What? Go back to sleep."

Delilah kept laughing, so hard now that tears were rolling down her face. "Snack mix! Pies! Coffee Cake! Desserts!"

"Delilah! Quiet!"

She turned and looked at Andy. It was a full moon and he could see an odd look in his wife's eyes. They were the eyes of someone he didn't know. Someone he didn't want to know.

"CRANBERRY SAUCE," she screamed "MORE RICE!"

It was after an hour of this that Andy called 911. When the ambulance arrived they found Delilah in the kitchen in her pajamas. Large bowls and casserole dishes filled the counter space. Delilah was emptying bags of sugar, flour and oil into them and onto the kitchen floor. She had just squished sticks of butter in her hands and onto her face. Containers of cinnamon and herbs lay empty on the Formica floor and she was laughing, eyes blazing.

The first medic called back to those coming up the rear. "It's another one men. Get the straight jacket."

"Another one?" asked Andy. Standing at a distance from the ruckus.

"PTFD."

"What?"

"Post Traumatic Food Disorder. T'is the season buddy. Okay men lets wrap her up."

Delilah mumbled a memorized recipe for cinnamon rolls as they carried her to the waiting ambulance.

# Joy to the Choir

By Stephanie Raffelock

It wasn't fair! For two years in a row, Cheryl McAdams got to be Mary and wear the blue veil and hold the baby Jesus doll in the Christmas Pageant. Cheryl McAdams stepped on my feet whenever she could, leaving black marks on my white socks and scuffs on my Mary Janes. When we were lined up, waiting to go into assembly, she would turn around stomp on my one of my feet, laugh, and then turn to the front of the line again like she hadn't done anything. No way she should have been Mary two years in a row!

I sang in the choir, directed by Mrs. Luella Pearson. Mrs. Pearson had bluish grey hair that she sprayed into a helmet on her head. Her face was heavily powdered. "Like a porcelain doll" my mother said, but I thought she looked more like a powdered donut.

Each year our school, which was a private school, a fact that my mother liked to share with relatives in a way that didn't make it private at all, put on a Christmas Pageant. The local television station invited the school to the studio and filmed the entire thing. It was the big event leading up to our winter break.

In parkas and scarves, boots and mittens we marched off of the school bus by grade, so bundled against the snow and cold that we looked like a little troop of Michelin men. Volunteer parents and teachers took us to dressing rooms where we were greeted by rows of freshly pressed, neatly hung choir robes. Sizes were found, parkas and boots were stashed and soon each kid had on a black robe with a white collar and a big red bow that tied under the collar.

Mrs. Pearson inspected us, standing in lines just that way that we would when we sang. She walked up and down, heels clicking on the concrete floor and gave us instruction.

"Be like angels," she said. "Look directly into the camera and smile your best smiles while you are singing. Remember that smiling helps to raise the note so that you do not sing flat."

Hearing these instructions, I vowed to hold them dear in the hopes that Mrs. Pearson might notice and cast me as Mary next year.

It cannot be easy for mere mortals to deal with 70 first through sixth graders. Our excitement was ramped up by the robust supply of cookies and candy, supplied by the television station. Like fat little puppies at the trough, we practically licked the floor when the sugary treats were gone.

The thing about so much sugar is that it makes kids think of doing things that they normally wouldn't do. Leonard, a boy from my class, had already eaten several cookies and quite a bit of candy. He regularly got in trouble at school. Leonard could bring class to a raucous stand still. He liked to put his hand in his armpit and then flap it like a wing in such a way as to make loud farting noises, bringing bouts of laughter. Girls were not supposed to laugh, but secretly I thought Leonard was a very funny kid.

Leonard was running around the television studio with the baby Jesus doll that he'd taken from the manger, and using it as a machine gun.

"Leonard, I told you last week, none of this nonsense! Stop all this fussing now. Do you want to do sit in the dressing room by yourself? Do you," she repeated, bending down and placing her hands on his shoulders. She straightened the large white collar on his choir robe, and fluffed the big red bow.

I was standing right next to them, so I saw all of it happen. Leonard listened to Mrs. Pearson with an intense look on his face and then a little smile. Mrs. Pearson straightened up and smiled back just as Leonard let rip a real fart. Loud, rolling and fragrant. Leonard started to laugh. All of the kids around him started to laugh. Mrs. Pearson turned whiter than the powder on her face and grabbed a handful of her helmet hair so hard that you could hear it crunch in her grip. For the rest of the day she had a dent on one side of her head.

Now Mrs. Pearson had to avoid Leonard because whenever he saw her, he started to laugh uncontrollably which brought on more laughter from other kids, except from the group of girls that included Cheryl McAdams, in her stupid looking blue Mary veil. They stood in their little pod and glared at Leonard.

"He is so rude," I heard one of them say.

"My mother would never let me play with him," said another

"Why would you want to?" chimed in Cheryl McAdams.

Finally it was time for the choir to line up and sing. The adults herded us to our places and we stood in two neat rows, kids in the back on risers so that everyone could be seen. Excitement bubbled over as bright lights shined down and a big camera focused on us. Mrs. Pearson stood behind the camera and raised her arms to direct our singing. I remembered what she had said about looking right into the camera and singing with a smile on your face.

We sang the Reader's Digest condensed version of the *Halleluiah Chorus* first. Then we sang *Away in a Manger*. Each time the camera went by I looked right into the lens, and without really meaning to, leaned slightly forward, as I smiled my best smile. What I didn't know at the time is that none of the other kids followed Mrs. Pearson's instructions, so they didn't look right into the camera. They didn't smile and none of them leaned forward as the camera went by.

As we came to the end of *Silent Night, Holy Night*, I leaned forward a little too far and fell onto my face taking three other kids out with me. It is to the cameraman's credit that he did not follow my descent with his lens-- and to Mrs. Pearson's credit that she didn't put another dent in her helmet hair. As I went down I could hear Leonard laughing uncontrollably.

On Christmas Eve my mother, my aunts, some cousins sat in our living room and watched the Christmas Pageant on television. My aunts were laughing and calling me a little ham. I scowled my best eight-year-old scowl and said, "I did exactly what Mrs. Pearson told us to do and I was the only one."

"You were definitely the only one sweetheart," said one of the aunts. With arms folded across my chest I continued to watch as I tumbled over the three kids that became part of the great *Silent Night* fall. Leonard could be heard laughing in the background. The screen faded to black and then to our principal, who with a sick look on her face wished everyone a "Very Merry Christmas and a Good Night."

Somewhere in another part of the city, a powdered Luella Pearson, replete with helmet hair was watching the Christmas Pageant too, and she was on her third martini.

# THE REAL GIFT

## BY *G.Z. Hill*

Taking a moment to look at the Christmas tree one more time, she leaned over and looked under the tree. Bent to the side and looked around the tree, then stopped and stared into the branches. She wasn't allowed over thirty minutes, and she had already taken twenty minutes and still hadn't found the clue.

Hands on hips she paused, her mouth pressed together in frustration, frowning and then she began pawing and poking, sneaking peeks at the tags one more time. She started to lift the packages, checking each side and tried to hurry. She searched the loaded branches with ornaments, dozens of hiding places and still she couldn't find it.

Nothing.

Nothing for Patti.

Patti sat on the floor, here hair brushing the

boughs sending red glitter down on top of her head as she checked each low hanging ornament. She glanced at Travis, who was smiling smugly, as he sipped hot buttered rum. She gave off a sigh, thinking . . . that at thirty years old she should be able to play this game a little faster.

She stared into the room, her eyes scanning the coffee table, the bookcase and the decorated pine boughs she had hung along the upstairs railing. She had been peeking and sneaking around for over a week, trying to get a head start on the game, but she couldn't find the clue.

She could feel Travis hiding his laughter. She glanced over and saw him looking at his watch. He was timing her, she was only allowed as many minutes as she was old. That was the game.

Standing up, she went back to looking inside the tree. It had to be hiding somewhere, somewhere deep in the branches. She looked over at him and he smiled, his bare foot bobbing up and down, watching and waiting, making a point of looking at his new watch, as he pretended to stretch his arms overhead, giving off a bored fake yawn.

"Babe, you're down to five minutes. Tick tock. Tick tock."

Patti looked some more then stepped back from the tree. She tried to think, *where would he put the clue? The tiny note or maybe a little box?*

"I'm going to count down, want me to tick tock off the last two minutes?"

"NO!" she parted the branches, lifting the shimmering garlands and fingered rolled the glass ornaments top to bottom. Over her shoulder she asked, "Did you cheat?"

"Nope." He smiled, "Keep looking, it's in plain sight."

She continued around the tree picking up ornaments and turning them over and then she stopped. On the bottom of a small antique glass tree that her grandmother had given her when she was a child, was a small squiggle. She took the ornament off the tree and looked at the bottom. She glanced at Travis but he was making a big show of checking his watch.

Turning the ornament every which way, she made out the faint outline of an arrow. She tried to remember how it was placed on the tree and then followed the arrow across the room to the window.

"Yes!" she screamed as she raced across the room, stopped and gasped. Outside, hanging from a tree branch was a box swinging by a gold cord. The falling

---

snow had almost covered it up. Next door, in her neighbor's driveway was a car with a large red bow. She looked at Travis, wondering if Mr. Grant was surprising his wife.

She knew the box had to be hers. They didn't have money for a new car. "How am I supposed to get it?"

Travis just shrugged. After sipping the last of his drink he stretched his arm and looked at his new watch and said, "Tick Tock."

"How much time?" she yelled, as she ran for the front door.

"Might give you a couple more minutes, but you'd better hurry."

She didn't take time to get a coat, but she slipped her feet into the boots that were sitting on the front porch. Racing around the house she looked up into the tree. *"Damn him. . ."* she muttered. She would need to go to the shed in the back yard and get a ladder.

She glanced at the car with the big red bow, and wondered, if maybe?

Travis walked over to the window and smiled, thinking of her dragging the ladder out of the shed and having to climb the tree. He watched as she scrambled through two inches of snow and pushed her way through the hedge to the Grants. He watched as she lifted the tag hanging off the red bow and glanced up at the window at him and frowned.

The tag was blank.

Travis lifted his refilled mug in a salute, pointing to the tree then pointed to his watch. He gave her a wave and watched as she crossed back over to their yard and followed the fence to the back garden shed.

Patti stared up into the tree as she passed under the snow heaped limbs. Snow was starting to come down in heavy wet flakes, soaking her as she carted the ladder across the lawn, leaving a wide track behind her. She set it up against the tree trunk, furious he had put the box so high. She looked up into the thick branches, wondering why he didn't just hang the box lower.

Travis watched as she adjusted the ladder. She glanced up to see if he was watching and then she took the first steps up into the wet branches. He couldn't see her open the box, but he watched the car next door. A moment later, he watched as she turned on the headlights and started the motor of the new Lexis.

He reached in the pocket of his pajamas for his own set of remote keys and clicked off the motor. He wanted her to go to the car and find the real gift sitting on the front seat.

Travis watched as she climbed out of the tree and stepped off the ladder and head back through the hedge to the car. Once again she switched on the remote, the headlights went on and the doors unlocked. She high stepped through the snow, lifting and dragging the edge of her wet nightgown, towards the car.

He smiled. He hoped she liked her real gift.

He watched her throw open the car door and lean inside. She pulled out a red Christmas blanket full of folds that dropped down to the wet snow. Peeking from her arms, through the folds of the blanket, was a puppy with soft brown eyes, wiggling and licking his wife's face in pure joy.

Patti glanced up at the window and smiled.

Travis felt a lump in his throat. Patti had never looked more beautiful to him, standing in the falling snow, her hair sprinkled with flakes, her nightgown wet and clinging to her legs as she leaned over and kissed the squirming puppy in her arms.

He smiled when she looked up towards the window and from the distance, he read her lips when she said, *I love you.*

Travis watched as she high stepped back across

her own tracks towards the house. The red blanket made a trail through the snow behind her, as she took off running. The puppy nestled tight against her neck continued to lick her face as she laughed.

He set down his cup and wondered if she would let him name the pup, Rudolph? He figured probably not, but he might ask anyway. He walked down the hall to the front door and waited for her to reach the porch.

"Merry Christmas Hon," he whispered into her neck as he gathered the two of them close. He felt the bulk of the blanket move and the squirming pup against his chest began to paw and lick his way toward his face. He looked down smiling and kissed her cold lips. "Merry Christmas."

Patti had told him earlier, she had one more gift for him. His real gift.

She looked up and smiled, "I have something to tell you."

He hoped she was going to tell him that they were finally pregnant.

# WHAT HAPPENS WHEN YOU LIE?

BY *G.Z.Hill*

I was told she was beautiful.

But how was I to know. I was only three years old when she was murdered.

It was not easy to get anyone to tell me about her death, or even what happened. It was as though the facts had been gathered up and forgotten, tucked away somewhere in the attic, in a box to be discussed when I got older.

Some other time. Or with luck, never.

As a young child, of course I was curious. I asked endless questions. Usually starting with, *where is my mother? Why don't I have a mother and father like Judy next door?*

No matter who I asked, the response was always the same. They would look away and leave out the details, and would only mumble that both my mother and father had died.

It was years later, when I learned what happened. Even then I didn't believe it and thought it must be a lie. A terrible lie. How could they accuse someone and let them take the blame. I was supposed to believe, because they told me so, that somehow my father was to blame. Maybe not directly . . .yet, everyone on my mother's side of the family wanted me to know that it was his fault. No one else's, no matter what the police said. It was my father that must have killed her.

My grandmother said, more than once. *Don't believe your grandmother Lu. She lives in New York, she wasn't even here when it happened. She doesn't know anything. Don't you go listening to her, yah hear?*

Everyone told me, when I was older, in a whispered voice. . .*your father was the one that killed her*, then as an afterthought would say, smiling, *I'm sure he didn't mean to.*

But I had to wonder. How could he do it? How could anyone? Why was everyone lying?

I remember when I came home from the first day of school, and I told my grandmother what everyone had said. I wondered how they knew what happened, and I didn't. How did everyone know what my father had done and how did they know what happened to my mother. Yet no one ever told me what had happened.

My grandmother looked away. That was the day everyone, in the family started to blame my father. He was the reason I didn't have a mother like Judy, next door. He was the reason, they said.

---

But somehow, I knew they were lying.

My father was also gone. Also dead.

I spent my childhood navigating the world of living with my grandmother, my mother's mother. Who, I should mention, tried her best, in her own way, to love me. But time played a trick on both of us, I started to look like my mother, act like my mother and some said I was a constant reminder of that terrible day when my mother had been found.

Sometimes I caught my grandmother looking at me in a funny way, as if she didn't like me, wanted me out of the house and to never come back. Other times she pretended. Pretended to like me, to like my friends, pretended that she was interested in my schoolwork, my sports and in my music. We both pretended. I knew she didn't care.

I often heard bits and pieces about what had happened to my mother. Each person recalling something almost forgotten, so that even though I hung on every word, I soon learned that memories and facts often didn't match.

It wasn't until I was older that I understood, that if I were to find out the truth, then I would need to find the truth for myself. That it wasn't possible to trust what everyone told me. I know they glossed over the details. Why tell me the truth? Why not just lie. Lying was so much easier.

As I got older I wondered who I could ask. Who would tell me the truth? I had no one. I was only three years old when my father killed himself. Some said it was guilt. My grandmother wouldn't speak of it and told me to let the ghosts go their way. She would scold me and tell me to stop asking questions. And then she would say, dropping her voice, *It was better to let the dead go in peace, no point in dragging the families dirty laundry back out for everyone to ask about again.*

Later I realized why they lied.

Why it was such a big secret.

It was because they knew the truth.

My grandmother packed up the house and moved us when I was in the fourth grade. She explained that the neighbors and the town would never forget, and that we needed to start over.

We moved to a town forty miles south, where my Aunt Josie, my mother's sister lived. Josie was on her third husband by the time I figured out that maybe she knew the truth.

When I asked, she would look away and say, *"Maybe later, when I have more time. . .when you are older."*

It didn't take me long to realize that Josie would never tell me the truth, or maybe it was just the drugs and the drinking that clouded her memories, but each story was woven with a string of maybes or might have happened, but mostly just all lies. She wouldn't even look at me when she tried to tell me what she thought had happened.

I was in the seventh grade when I figured out that Josie resented our living so close. She seldom visited us and was never home when we went to see her, although her car would be parked in the driveway and we could see the TV flickering through the half-slit blinds.

It didn't take me long to figure out that Josie hated her mother, my grandmother. Hated what happened. Then I began to wonder why?

My grandmother never mentioned my mother. All pictures had been packed away and never unpacked, when we moved the last time.

I insisted on keeping one picture.

It was one of my mother holding my hand in front of Saint Mary's at Easter. We both wore matching wide brimmed straw hats with daises tucked in the ribbon band. My mother's flowered dress fluttered in the wind, one gloved hand held down her billowing skirt, the other held my white gloved hand, as I flattened my hat down from blowing away.

We both smiled into the camera.

I have no memory of her. Of that Easter.

No memory of that day at all, but I have a picture of a beautiful woman smiling as my father took that picture of the two of us as we left Mass that Sunday morning.

The only reason I had that picture was because my grandmother Lu, in New York, had saved it for me. She had others of my father but that was the only one I had of my mother with me.

I was going into my junior year in High School when I asked my grandmother to tell me the truth. To tell me what happened to my mother. I remember that afternoon vividly. I was full of myself, feeling very grown up, as I demanded to know what everyone knew but me. I wanted to know what happened on that night in August, when the police found my mother at the lake, where her body had washed ashore.

Both hands had been chopped off.

I felt very grown up, as I stared her down, demanding to hear the truth, all the while, fighting back tears, watching her face crumble in shock.

As if I slapped her, I watched the color drain from her powdered cheeks and her eyes fill with tears, glazing over the cataracts that were stealing her sight. If I could have taken back the words, the tone and the way I spoke, I would have, but it was too late.

The silence that filled the room and the shock that pushed her deep into the old rocker that suddenly stilled from her shifting weight made me realize that maybe I had been wrong.

Looking up, her eyes widened, as if seeing me for the first time as a young woman. Maybe as a spitting image of my mother when she was a teenager. I seemed to take her breath away.

My grandmother's head nodded in a slow sweep as she took a deep breath, gathering some inner strength as if knowing that this day had finally come.

As if knowing that someday I would find out the truth anyway. She didn't smile as her voice dropped to a whisper, then glanced away. "I promise I will tell you everything. But not tonight."

She picked up the Better Homes and Garden magazine, dismissing me as she flipped open the pages. "Maybe when you are older, you'll understand." She called after me, when I turned.

I remember walking out of the room and up the stairs to my small attic bedroom. In another week I would be sixteen. I would have my driver's license and then I could go to the police and ask to see the records. I figured maybe 16 was how old I needed to be to finally hear the truth. To see the public records. If not 16, then I'd wait until I was 18. Either way, I wouldn't need my grandmother to tell me anything. I would never ask her again.

As I flopped on my bed, I couldn't help but wonder what my mother had done to have her hands chopped off, and why my father killed himself on the same day they found her?

And would the police even talk to me now because they might consider me a kid. I wanted to know the truth, but what I really want to know was why?

## CHRISTMAS EVE- 10 years later

I watched my grandmother lay between the neatly folded sheets, the machines ticking and clicking with the sighs of air filling her lungs. I watched the slow drips from her IV, pushing drugs into her blue ropey veins, giving her the fluids she needed to live. Her face sunken, with wrinkles.

I had come a long way to find out the truth.

I wondered if she would tell me what happened. There was still time for her to do as she had promised. Still time to tell me her version of what happened in August all those many years ago.

I knew my grandmother had lied.

She had lied about everything.

My grandmother, who raised me out of guilt, had lied from the very beginning.

I dropped her thin hand, when the nurse pulled back the curtain in a fast clang of chains as the fabric rolled along the track that curved overhead around her bed. I could see into the hallway, where the lights were still on, but now seemed dimmer than when I had arrived two hours earlier. Across from her door was a fake bough with holly sprigs hanging off a plastic red bow.

The nurse managed a brief smile as she moved around the bed. She looked down at my grandmother, then turned away and checked the IV lines, moving dials on the monitor next to the bed.

She glanced at me and whispered, "I can bring you a cot, if you would like."

"No, the chair is fine." I tried smiling, but knew that I wouldn't be sleeping. I had no intention of spending the night, not unless it was necessary. I traveled across two states. I was here for one reason and one reason only. I had a plan.

"Let me bring you a pillow and some blankets." The nurse eased past the curtain, yanking it closed in another metal scrape along the track, shutting out the lights from the hall.

I could hear her steps slap down the hallway away from the door. Further way there were murmurs of voices that drifted from the nurse's station, then somewhere, in another room, I heard a telephone ring. Then silence.

My grandmother's room held little signs of Christmas. A few cards were set-aside on the wide windowsill. I noticed that none of them had been opened, probably because Josic hadn't been by in several days. Across the room, over the white dry erase board someone had tacked up a string banner that read Happy Holidays. It was a sad reminder and I wanted desperately to yank it down.

It was Christmas Eve. I wondered how many others were sitting in hospitals like me, holding someone's hand and watching the clock wishing they were somewhere else. Just sitting, waiting and watching the machines. Wondering how much time was left and wondering if this would be their last Christmas together.

When I flew over the city late in the afternoon, I wondered how other families managed when people they loved were no longer here to celebrate Christmas, when they were gone and wouldn't be coming back. When all that was left was memories. Except I didn't even have that.

I thought about my own family. How much I missed them and wished I were back home.

Inside my leather briefcase were copies of various reports. The pages were now dog-eared, worn and smudged from all the times I tried to read between the lines, trying to make sense of what had happened. The pages were incomplete because the case had never been solved.

No one had been arrested for killing my mother. The police had said that her case was now in the Cold Case files, but they assured me, if there was new evidence the case would be reopened.

I opened my notebook and scanned down the list of questions I had asked the retired detective that had been the first to handle my mother's case. It had taken some time to find him, but when I did, he answered my questions patiently, and when I could think of nothing else to ask, he had a few questions of his own.

Even though the case was over twenty years old, he did remember my mother. He remembered my father, he especially remembered meeting my grandmother, and had remembered what she had told him.

When he offered to drive down from Mt. Hood and meet with me, I had little hope that he would remember anything more than what we had talked about on the phone. I told him that my grandmother was dying and had little time left.

He was quiet a moment, and then insisted on driving down to the city. He said it didn't matter that it was Christmas Eve, that he would like to meet me and that he had some questions for her. He asked me to call him when I got to the hospital.

Now watching her as she was drifting off to the other place, I wondered what purpose it would serve if she did wake up. Would she tell me the truth after all these years?

She was dying. She had heart failure and the cancer that was growing in her brain, was erasing her memory as it twisted and killed cells, maybe eating away the truth of what happened.

I was baking sugar cookies when she called.

She asked me to come. Said it was important and she wanted to set things right with the Lord. She promised that she would tell me everything if I would just come, and would hurry. She wanted to die in peace knowing that she had done the right thing and she had said it was time, I heard what happened. Heard what really had happened.

I had been stunned by the call. She was sobbing, when I told her I'd check flights. I hung up and went back to baking cookies, wondering if leaving my family during Christmas would serve any purpose. Was this just another time she would lie? Thinking I would come because she was dying.

So I came. After three years away, I came because I needed to find out why she lied. I forced myself to wait for her to wake up. Forced myself to hold her hand and watch the machines hoping that she would know I was with her, and would wake up. Thinking about all the other Christmas Eve's in the past, I knew that this would be our last together.

Then thinking about it, as I had so many times in the past. I made a decision.

I leaned over and pulled the plugs on the machines that were keeping her alive. I watched the clock and then watched the machines go dark. I watched her chest rise and fall for the last time and then stop. I listened to the silence, then gathered my things and stood.

The police could never prove it, but they suspected her of killing them both.

I picked up my brief case and walked away from the bed, then stood in the doorway to her room and watched as the nurse rushed down the hallway. In her arms were blankets and a pillow, she was bringing for me. Her eyes were wide as she rushed past me towards the bed. I could hear other's calling out as two more nurses rounded the hall corner and ran towards me.

I glanced around, to make sure that I had plugged in the monitor and then started to cry.

Because-

That's what you do. That's what's expected when someone you love dies.

You cry.

I didn't cry for her.

I cried for my mother and father.

I watched as the nurse lifted her cold wrist and felt for a pulse, then she gave me a sad nod.

I moved into the hallway, expecting the nurse to call me back, or to call for security, instead when nothing happened, I walked to the elevator.

I dialed the detective. No need for him to make that long trip into the city on Christmas Eve. I thought he needed to be home with his family.

After all these years we both would never really know what happened. The nurse had told me that sometimes patients do wake up. Sometimes.

But I knew if she did she would just lie.

I had promised my girls that I would be home in time for them to unwrap their presents in the morning. Now I could catch the next flight out of PDX like I had planned.

I gripped the phone, feeling a sense of relief when he answered. I told him that my grandmother was gone, and I was sorry to tell him, that she would be taking her secrets to the grave.

He sounded disappointed when he asked, "What happened?"

I told him the truth.

She suddenly stopped breathing.

# THE BENCH

## BY *G.Z. Hill*

Art slipped onto the seat of the van, next to Gaynor, and glanced around to make sure that no one was listening.

Gaynor smiled, "You got your list?"

Art nodded, patting the pocket of his blue jacket. "Did Esther give you a long list?"

"Nope. You?"

"See's candy." Art watched the van drive through the gate of The Willows Retirement Home.

Neither man said another word as the van took the road out of the residential neighborhood then passed the hospital and clinics that everyone seemed to visit on a regular schedule. The van drove slowly, along the route, careful of bumps, as it headed to the shopping mall downtown.

The chatter from the women in the rows behind them couldn't be heard, because both men refused to wear their hearing aids when they went to the mall on Saturday.

Art insisted that the aids made him look old.

Gaynor didn't want to look like the old fart sitting on the bench next to Art, so he stuffed his in his pocket, so Esther wouldn't know he had taken them out.

When the van reached the mall, the driver announced that he would be back in two hours. The women chatted away, canes and walkers tapping their way into the mall entrance, while Art and Gaynor left the women in a rush to get inside. Both headed for the motorized carts waiting inside the entrance, both got lucky. There were four sitting in a row waiting to be used. Both hurried before the women arrived knowing that one of them would insist they give one up for a change.

Art turned to Gaynor, as they both grabbed a cart. "I want to go to See's Candy first, then we can meet at the bench."

Gaynor nodded. "I have to go to the other end of the mall and pick up something for Esther, at Macy's, so I'll meet you when I'm finished." Both took off, slowly easing through the holiday shoppers and at the big Y, under the clock, each went a different direction.

Both in a hurry.

Both looking forward to spending some time on the bench. Neither checked the time, as they hurried to get their shopping done. The most important part of the morning was not the shopping, nor the lunch, but getting to the bench as soon as possible. Getting to the bench before anyone else.

After a long line at See's Art handed over Hanna's meticulous list of numbers and addresses, then he handed over his credit card, hoping she hadn't decided to spend four hundred dollars like she did last year. How in the hell you could spend that much on chocolates beat the shit out of him, but she somehow managed. She told him it was easier than shopping and *to just deal with it.*

She would spend hours looking at the catalog and then wasted more time asking him what he thought, and then wanted him to help her decide what to order for each one on the list. He hated that part of it, but he didn't mind going to See's Chocolates in the mall, once she had her list in order because that meant time on the bench.

The clerk, took his time going over the numbers and after what seemed an eternity, he rang up the total. The charges only totaled three hundred and twenty four dollars. Art smiled. That meant she had forgotten someone.

It also meant another visit to the mall. He grabbed his credit card and rushed his cart back into the mall and beeped his way through shoppers as he headed for the bench.

Gaynor had got to the bench first and was annoyed that a woman with her two kids were hogging up all the space. He pulled his cart close hoping she wasn't planning on sitting there all morning. The two boys, with their jumping and racing around in front of the bench were starting to piss him off. With his hearing aids out he couldn't hear them but he had been looking forward all week to just sitting quietly and watching the shoppers, what he didn't need was the damn distraction.

Art putzed his scooter from the other end of the mall and could see Gaynor in the distance. He scowled hoping those damn kids and the heavyset woman, who was sprawled on his bench didn't plan to sit there very long. By the time he reached Gaynor she was picking up her shopping sacks and shouting to the boys to settle down. .

Art wheeled close to Gaynor and faced the shops across the wide hallway. People were streaming by in a crushing sea of shopping bags, so many shoppers that it was hard to see into the shops. There were women in pairs, young girls texting and walking, a few couples together and some mothers pushing strollers but it was the women going in and out of the store across from the bench they wanted to see.

"To damn many people," Gaynor mumbled.

Art handed him a small sack of candy. "I spent so much money, that these are all the free samples. Help yourself."

Gaynor peeked in the sack and lifted out a hard square. "Is this a damn caramel?"

"How would I know?"

Gaynor nibbled at the hard square, licking off the chocolate coating and then dropped it back in the sack.

"What hell did you do that for?" Art grabbed the sack, and pulled out the soggy piece.

"It would have stuck in my dentures."

Art dropped the candy to the floor and wiped his hands on his jacket. If he sat just right, he could look into the store through the wide entrance every time there was a gap in the walkers streaming by. There were so many Christmas shoppers that it was hard to focus on any one display.

Art smiled. "Did you see that one?"

Gaynor nodded then pointed to the front windows. "Changed the display since we were here last."

"They also moved the bras up to the front."

"Yep." Gaynor thought a moment and tried to remember the last time Esther had worn a bra.

Art tilted his head towards Gaynor. "This is my favorite time of year. Look at all those beauties shopping for new undies."

Gaynor smiled. "Did you check out the garters to the left?"

"Does a bear shit in the woods?"

Both men chuckled as they settled down and watched the women pass in and out of the doors of store with their pink shopping bags.

Neither noticed their wives, who had arrived by taxi, sitting in Starbucks two shops down.

"So this is where the old goats go every Saturday." Hanna said. After seeing enough of the nonsense, she stood. Opened her walker and waited for Esther to stand. "What do you say we go to Victoria's Secret and spend their money?"

"And buy what?" Esther mumbled. She hadn't worn a bra in years and truth be known, she didn't much like the idea of starting now, at eighty-five.

Hanna stopped, turned and asked. "Do you think they even have anything in there that will fit us?"

"Speak for yourself Hanna, I'm still a size ten!"

Hanna sucked in her stomach, and threw back her shoulders. *Well la de dah*! She at least still wore a bra! With that, she thumped her walker forward, neither looking left or right.

Both marched by the bench and entered the store without looking back.

If they had, they would have seen two old men start their scooters and hurry through the crowd towards the food court.

# IS IT YOU?

## BY *G.Z. Hill*

**"I didn't plan for it to happen but I couldn't stop."**

*Today I saw her walk into the Garden Plaza with her Macy's bags swinging against her red skirt each step making her dress flare out exposing her long tanned legs. I watched as the winter coat and scarf floated in the wind, then stared at the red-strapped high heels begging for someone to knock her down.*

*I would never forget her, although I had spent six months trying.*

*There she was. It was her!*

*The one that started it all. . .*

*The one I thought I killed.*

Horns honked behind him. First one. Then a

---

second. Then several horns started an angry chorus beeping him into traffic, forcing him to drive back up to speed through the intersection.

His hands gripped the wheel as he stared into the rear view mirror, watching the Garden Plaza slip away behind him down the block. He turned on his blinker, forcing his way into the right lane to toots of horns. Flipping the bird over his shoulder, to the other driver he made his way slowly, behind bumper-to-bumper traffic to the end of the block.

Muttering, as he pounded the steering, over and over he screamed.

*Damn her*! Damn! Damn!

His hands trembled as he turned right and headed down the block. He fought the rush of bile rising in his throat as panic consumed him at seeing the ghost. He kept muttering, *there is no way it's her. No way in hell.*

He circled the block and parked across the street from the Garden Plaza, letting the motor run as he stared up into the windows that climbed ten stories into the snow threatening sky from the sidewalk.

*It couldn't be her!*

He pulled down the rear view mirror and stared into the dirty glass. He had changed. The mustache, the lightened hair even the fake glasses made him look different. He was different. Then he smiled, he was getting better.

He flipped the mirror back in position and watched the entrance as people rushed through the glass doors into the lobby. Inside the foyer was a massive tree decorated in white twinkling lights behind large silver and crystal balls. It was a far cry from the fake tree his mother had set on top of their old Sony TV. He squeezed his eyes shut. He didn't want to think of his mother.

Then he opened them and began watching the shoppers as they passed. He wondered if the woman was visiting family or friends. Maybe just dropping off gifts for someone she knew. Maybe it wasn't even her.

He pounded the steering wheel.

It couldn't have been *her*. . .but, then again. . .

Maybe he didn't kill her. Maybe he just thought she was dead. She had no pulse, he had checked. He shook his head, nope, not her. Someone that just looked like her, fooled his eyes when he caught a fast glimpse of her as she turned the corner. But it was the red hair. That dammed red hair! How many women had that color of hair? How many?

Again he smiled, because he was always looking.

His fists clenched at the thought of another mistake as he looked out and noticed that it had started to snow. Glancing at his watch, he noticed the time. He would need to hurry. The train would be due in another twenty minutes. With the start of snow, the one he had found, may need a ride. He hit the blinker and nosed the taxi back into the rush hour traffic.

His heart flipped up a beat as he switched on the Out Of Service light. Ignoring people that stepped off the curb into the street to wave him down, he looked away whipping the taxi around drivers that were too slow. He needed to hurry. He needed to be there waiting. He needed to see her, to be sure, to be certain that she was the one. The one he had watched floating.

His cell rang on the seat beside him. It would be his mother, reminding him to pick up the canned cranberry jelly she wanted for Christmas dinner. He let the cell ring, knowing she would be angry but it was the sixth time she had called in the last hour. Yapping about *when are you coming home? Will you be on time for dinner? Did you remember to* pick up *the cranberry?* On and on.

Clenching his jaw he fought the rage at being stuck with her, of having to take care of her. He cast a fast glance to the floor of the taxi where a lone can of cranberry jelly rolled back and forth against the empty coke cups and crumpled fast food sacks. Rolling and reminding him that he had to go home.

For the moment, all he could think about was the woman.

Couldn't believe it was her. Couldn't be!

Gripping the steering wheel, he concentrated on driving across town, honking his way in and out of traffic. He had to hurry.

Now there were two mistakes, two problems. He slammed his hands on the steering wheel in frustration. He thought he had killed them both. He was sure of it. Certain of it.

There was no way both could have lived.

Except he knew that one did.

One that was just getting on a train to hurry home.

~~~

## HAS HE FOUOND ME?

Marcie Lang raced across the lobby of the Plaza. She flashed a smile to Ronald, the doorman, and asked, "Any messages?" as she shifted the three shopping bags from one hand to the other.

"No Miss Lang." He smiled and noticed the bags, "Do you need help with those?"

She shook her head no, rushing across the marble floor, her heels clicking as she rushed to the elevators. Turning, giving him a smile, she said, "Merry Christmas." Then hurried to push the button for her floor.

"You too Miss Lang."

Marcie hurried into the elevator, sinking back against the brass rail and tried to take deep breaths, to calm her racing heart. She willed herself to breath slowly. To take a deep breath letting the air whisper out as she felt the elevator lift her up from the lobby to the soft hum of the motor. She watched the numbers flash and then stop on six to the apartment she now called home.

Shifting the shopping bags, filled with last minute gifts she wondered why she had waited until the last minute. It had been stupid, everyone was in a rush, adding to her panic. Glancing down into the three bags she wondered if she had bought enough. Checks were fine, but children expected presents. Pretty boxes filled with things they had been wanting, and wishing for, not just stuff pulled off a shelf in a hurry. She shifted the bags and could see a jumble of assorted books and games inside. Now realizing her mistake, she should have called her sister for ideas of what they wanted. They probably had already read the books and had the games. Now they would be disappointed.

Today had been the second time she had attempted to go out alone. The day before she only made it to the end of the block before she raced back to the safety of the Plaza where Arnold had been waiting for her, throwing open the door then watched as she ran back to the elevators.

Arnold knew why she hurried inside. He looked outside, wondering if he was out there. He stood at the doors and watched the taxi's pass by.

Today she had made the three blocks. Too close to get a taxi, but too far to walk. After several hesitations at the lobby door she pushed her way outside and hurried into the protection of other shoppers as she headed for Macy's. Each step forced her close to the front of shops where she wanted to rush inside for protection. When she entered Macy's she felt such an overwhelming sense of relief that she had collapsed at the perfume counter and pretended she wanted to test samples.

She smiled. Today had been a milestone. Three blocks!

Tomorrow she would get a taxi. Arnold would call one for her and watch her slip inside. There would be no more excuses. Marci was expected be at the house first thing in the morning when the girls opened their gifts around the Christmas tree. She didn't want Peter, her brother-in-law, to leave the family and come get her again.

It was time she started doing things for herself, time she stopped worrying about him finding her.

Marcie stepped on the threshold of the elevator, using her bags to keep the doors open as she looked down the hall. Looking both ways, she could see that the hall was empty. No one was waiting for her. Taking a deep breath she hurried across the plum colored carpet and took off running.

Gripping her keys tightly, she pulled them out of the pocket of her coat, glancing behind her as she opened the door and rushed inside. She dropped the shopping bags, then quickly locked the door. Securing the additional two dead bolts that had been installed four months earlier.

Punching in the security code, she sank against the door taking huge gulping breaths, trying to stop the hammering in her chest. She hated being so scared all the timed. Hated the feeling of being watched. Hated being trapped.

After a moment she picked the shopping bags off the floor and walked down the hall to her bedroom, glancing into each room as she passed, making sure she was alone.

She knew she was safe. She was home. She had actually walked three blocks alone. She took a deep breath and smiled as she entered her bedroom.

Alexander, her Persian cat, looked up from the pile of pillows against the headboard and stretched when she walked towards the bed. He gave off a soft meow when she tossed her leather tote on the bed, then she dumped the shopping bags upside down, spilling out games and books over the bed. He gave a high stepping dance across the books towards her.

"Hey Alex, did you guard the place for me?" she bent over, rubbing his head then she cupped his face and kissed his whiskered cheek as she sank on the bed and kicked out of her red shoes.

Inside her leather tote, her cell rang. Marci smiled as she dug inside, scooping Alex over to her lap she answered. "Hey there."

Holly laughed. "You did great."

"I was terrified."

"I know. . ." Holly nodded to Arnold as she passed, mouthing *Merry Christmas*. "But you knew I was right behind you the whole time."

"But I never saw you."

"That was the whole idea." Holly reached the

elevator and punched the button for seven.

"Are you coming by?"

"No, I'm going to go upstairs first, but I'll be down later and bring some wrapping paper and ribbon, do you need anything else?"

Marcie looked at the last minute gifts, thinking that everything looked pretty lame, wishing she had spent more time and bought the girls something to wear. "Can you come now?"

Holly rolled her eyes. "I'll be down soon, and I'll call you when I head for the elevator so you know I'm on my way."

Marcie nodded to herself as she hung up.

She had to stop depending on Holly and take back her life. Everyone was getting tired of having to stop their life to babysit her all the time.

Walking over to the bedroom window she peeked through the folds of the satin drapes and looked down to the street below. There were dozens of taxi's passing in and out of traffic. Cars starting to turn on their lights in the early dusk of evening, she had got home just in time. Before it turned dark.

It was Christmas Eve, people were in a hurry to get home and meet friends after work. She wanted to stay home tonight. To stay safe.

Gripping the drapes, Marcie fought a wave of panic as she watched one taxi after another pull next to the sidewalk in front of shops down the block. People were running into the street waving to catch a ride. Everyone in a hurry, rushing towards the taxi's as snow started to fall out of the sky in fat lazy flakes.

"Be careful," she whispered, as she watched a lone woman step off the curb and wave.

*He's out there somewhere.* Driving his taxi. Looking for another woman.

She let the curtain fall back in place and took a deep breath. She was safe. She had moved. There was nothing to fear. Not anymore.

Why be so afraid? He thought she was dead.

~~~~~~~~

## CAN YOU SEE ME?

Across town in another building, was another woman muttering to herself.

*Double-check the locks.*

*Double check that the keys are in my pocket.*

Nance heard her own voice cut through the stillness. She turned from the hall mirror in her entry, catching a fast glimpse of her face covered by a long fringed blue knit scarf. A scarf that hid the scar on her right cheek where she wrapped it over her head, and under her chin, covering most of her face.

She hurried down the hall past the darkened living room, where only one light was shining on the side table, by the fireplace. The drapes were pulled shutting out the afternoon light. The room was spacious, filled with art from all over the world, a reminder of her other life, and all the trips she had taken over the years. A reminder of the freedom she used to enjoy.

The room looked unlived in, because it was.

Nance took off her gloves, shifting her Bulgari handbag from one hand to the other. Stuffing the gloves in the pocket of her coat, she walked towards the light coming from the bedroom down the hall. Then she stopped. *No!*

Jerking the keys out of her coat pocket she turned and walked back to the entry. Every day it was the same things, forcing herself to remember. To do things the same way, every day, so she could find things again, keep track of her keys, know where her cell phone was. Trying to remember had been hell. Exhausting and frustrating, but she knew she was doing better. Once more, like the hundred times a day she did it, she patted the left pocket of her slacks.

Nance knew she was getting better, but it was taking to long for her to recover her memory loss, and even though she was told that it might be temporary, and that she might start remembering, she was also reminded that her injuries were extensive. Head trauma was tricky, healing took time and sometimes, full recovery of events may not happen. She was determined to try. To prove them wrong, that she would regain her memory, she had to.

So every day she tried to remember what the hell he looked like.

Gripping the keys, Nance walked down the hall to the entrance and this time she didn't look into the mirror as she opened the drawer of the credenza, from Africa. Instead she dropped the keys into the enameled box inside. She walked away, then turned around to make sure that she had closed the drawer. Smiling, she remembered to close it. That was a first! Maybe she was getting better, maybe she would remember.

She walked back towards her bedroom. Her long coat was damp from the pelting snow that hurled its way out of the dark sky a she walked, home from the train station. The bottom edge of her slacks was now soggy and mud spattered from her walk from the train station to her home.

With each step, down the carpeted hall she could feel the heavy drag along the bottom of her coat and could hear the wet slapping sound of it flapping against her pant legs.

Nance felt relieved to be home, to be back behind locked doors. For months she rarely left her home unless it was essential and only on the good days. The days she felt strong enough to check each driver, of each taxi, as it slowly passed her. To see if she would remember him, if she caught a glance of the one that had driven her off into the night and tried to kill her.

Today had been a good day.

People were happy. Christmas Eve shoppers had filled the train with their loaded shopping bags. Children, wide-eyed looked outside the rushing windows as the train passed the stores decorated with Christmas displays and twinkling lights. Decorations hung on the lamp poles as the train flashed down the track. Off in the distance on the far hillside, homes were outlined in colored lights, Christmas trees with lights glowing could be seen in windows and in front yards as the commuter train rumbled from station to station dumping and gathering people in a rush to escape the ride and hurry home.

Nance had listened to children's voices talk about

Santa, about Christmas parties, and about opening presents. She couldn't help but smile as she heard snatches of conversations bubble all around her. She remembered loving this time of year. It was fun surprising the people she loved with gifts.

She remembered the parties she had given and all those she had gone to, over the years at friends' homes where once you opened the front door, you were greeted by the smells of cinnamon and vanilla. Where everyone lifted their glasses and hugged a greeting with Merry Christmas and a brush of a kiss. Where beautiful packages where tucked under the tree to be opened later.

This year would be different.

Nance slipped off her coat and tossed it across the bed as she leaned over and unzipped her boots kicking then off. Realizing what she had just done, she pulled the wet coat off the bed and walked back down the hall to the entry closet. Hanging up the coat, she was careful to leave plenty of room between the hangers so her coat could dry. Halfway down the hall she turned around and noticed that she had forgot to close the closet door.

She took a deep breath and glanced into the darkened living room and paused. She used to love entertaining in this room, with the sweeping view of the hills and downtown. But that was before. Now when she had company her friends never stayed along when they stopped by to check on her. No one spoke about what happened, until they got ready to leave and then, with eyes flitting away from her scared face, they would ask, their voice dropping, if the police had caught him yet.

No Christmas tree trimmed in the corner of her high ceilinged living room. No stacks of presents for her to deliver or to open, no cards waiting in her home office to be address and mailed. This Christmas she had turned down the parties, and the trips out of town to visit family. This year it was all about trying to remember. Trying to remember what the hell he looked like so she could help the police find the man that left her for dead.

The only reminder of the holiday was the massive floral arrangement that the office had sent her, with a card scrawled with everyone's well wishes and cheery notes. The arrangement sat in the middle of the glass dining table at the far end of the long living area. Dozens of red roses and green boughs scented the room.

It had arrived two weeks earlier, but now the needles were falling onto the glass top and the roses drooped, needing water. The candles jutting out of the middle remained unlit and also forgotten. Every time she glanced towards that end of the room she was reminded that she was their boss and they were waiting for her to return to work. She would, she vowed, after New Year's.

Nance was thankful that she had enough wits about her to have her attorney, set up fat bonus packages, and arrange for a catered holiday buffet to be delivered to the office. This year there would be no gala year-end party at one of the hotel ballrooms for the staff and their clients. She knew that they understood. What they didn't know, was that she didn't want anyone to climb into another taxi until he was caught.

Nance stepped onto the white living room carpet, pulling off the damp scarf that covered her head. She touched the raw rippled edge of the scar that needed another skin graft. Taking a deep breath she crossed the dimly lit living area. The lone lamp cast a path of light next to the floor to ceiling window. The light was on for a reason. Every night, since she had been released from the hospital, she had done the same thing.

She willed herself to cross the room and stand in the light.

Without hesitation she walked over to the floor to ceiling windows and draw back the drapes. With each tug of the fabric rushing open she willed herself to stand in the open and gaze down to the street below. The one light in the room, exposed her as she watched the shoppers below as they walked, head bent into the falling snow.

The evening traffic was bumper to bumper slow, with cars inching along the slick street as taxicabs pushed their way close to the curb looking for shoppers loaded with bags, needing a ride.

She glanced up into the gray sky and saw another swirling flurry of flakes fall heavily, coating the sky in polka dots drifting down starting to stick on the roofs of the cars below. The sky had threatened to snow all day and it was finally happening. She imagined children everywhere, looking out their windows watching the snow fall.

In the distance she could see red light flickers of cars bumper-to-bumper crawling over the bridges in the distance, crossing the river to the other side of the city. People would be rushing home to get ready for Christmas Eve parties, baking last minute cookies, wrapping gifts and helping children write letters to Santa.

Nance didn't want to think about what everyone else was doing. She had to do what she did every night. She willed herself to stand in the light. She could be seen if anyone looked up. If anyone was interested in the woman who stood in the window above the Sugar & Spice Bakery on Fifth.

She stood close to the glass wanting him to know she hadn't moved. To let him think she had remembered.

To remind him, he had made a mistake.

Like so few others. She had lived. The police needed her to remember what he looked like. She tried, but there was a blank hole in her memory where he had pounded her skull with a brick, then used his knife on her face. The Doctors reminded her that forgetting what happened, with that kind of trauma was common. Understandable. It would take time to recover. Maybe, not remembering what happened was her way of surviving.

She felt the prickle of unease, as she gazed below, knowing he was out there. Watching. Waiting. She wanted him to know that she wasn't afraid.

Looking down into the street below, across from her building, was a taxi parked next to the curb. She wondered if the driver was watching her stand at the window. If he was looking up and watching her. If it was him was he hoping that she would be stupid enough to climb into his taxi for the last time?

She couldn't remember his face today Maybe tomorrow? Maybe the day after? But for now, she only remembered the rough touch of his hands as he threw her to the ground, his smell, the weight of his body. She still remembered hitting the rocks near the river and rolling down the bank. The water. The cold wet wind on her bloody face. The black rushing pain as she felt herself floating over rocks into the thick slime of foam reeking of death.

Then sweet nothing.

Now she wished she had paid attention to what he looked like when she got in the taxi. Why didn't she ever look up from her work and pay attention to the driver? Why in the hell had she been so sidetracked that night?

She watched the stream of traffic then looked back at the lone taxi waiting at the curb as she whispered into the glass, "You made a mistake."

Nance pressed closer, as her hand touched the cold glass. Her reflection bounced back into the room, forcing her to see the damage. She lifted her hand and traced the ridged welt on her check, wincing from the tender line. She looked away. It was hard to see what she now kept hidden under a long scarf. Hard to see what he had done to her, but she wanted him to see. She wanted him to know that it didn't matter. She had lived.

She shifted forward exposing her bald head, where her long red hair had been shaved away for surgery. Her hand smoothed over her head, feeling the start of prickly hair trying to grow. A red line could still be seen as it circled up over her ear across her skull towards her forehead as she moved closer into the light.

Looking down to the street below, watching cars drive down the one-way street Nance noticed that the lone taxi remained at the curb. Sitting there, lights off. Waiting. Like so many other nights, it's out of service light was on. She could see exhaust steam into the cold night air as the car's motor idled.

Could it be him, she wondered. Was he even out there somewhere? She stared across the street to the lone taxi. The one she had seen before sitting at the curb, so many nights before. She whispered into the glass, "Can you see me?"

As if he knew. As if he could hear her.

Her mouth curved into a smile as she watched the headlights of the taxi, flash on and off. Then she watched as the taxi pulled away from the curb and nosed slowly back into the flow of traffic.

Pressing her hand to the window, she watched as he crossed under her window. For the first time the numbers were clear. "You just fucked up." She whispered. Nance took her finger and smeared across the cold glass, the number of his taxi she could read off the roof of the car. She pulled her cell out of the pocket of her slacks, dialing the private number she knew by heart and watched as the taxi's tail lights sat locked in traffic, waiting for the light to change at the end of the block.

Nance patted her left pocket, like she did a hundred times a day. She heard the ringing, and waited for the Detective to answer, wondering if he was home with his family or on his way home. Wondering if he was busy buying last minute gifts for his two boys or if she was calling him in the middle of another investigation.

She stared into the falling snow and listened to the phone ring and ring and ring and ring. . .hoping that he was waiting for her to call like he had promised. She could hear church bells in the background when he answered.

"Is it him?" he asked, then was silent a moment, waiting for her to answer, then asked. "Do you think it's him?"

Nance smoothed her hand over her shaved head and stared at the reflection of herself in the glass, not sure how to answer.

"Did he flash his headlights like before?" He asked.

"Yes." She looked down into the street and watched a woman at the next block wave a taxi over to the sidewalk. She leaned into the glass, but couldn't read the number on the roof of the taxi. Couldn't be sure, but she felt her heart race as the woman disappeared into the backseat.

"Nance, did he follow you home?"

"He follows me everywhere."

She couldn't identify him. Didn't know his face, but she knew his touch, knew his smell. "I have the number of his taxi." She read off the numbers she had written on the window and added, "I think he just picked up another woman on the next block."

The Detective lowered his voice, "I'll call it in, are you sure it's him?"

She hesitated. Her hand dropped inside the left pocket of her slacks, and as she had done a hundred times a day, she gripped the gun as she answered. "I don't know. Maybe."

"Don't leave, don't go anywhere until we pick him up."

She pulled the gun from her pocket and checked the chamber. Holding and enjoying the weight of it, the power it had. She wondered about the woman that got in the back seat of the taxi down the block. If only she had climbed in his taxi at the train station maybe she could have saved the woman with red hair. . But then. . .if she had. . .She would never have forgiven herself if she had killed the wrong man on Christmas Eve.

Slipping the gun back in her pocket she looked

across the street and noticed a man, standing next to his taxi, looking up. She couldn't see his face through the falling snow, but she knew it was him.

Her hand slowly lifted the gun.

The snow fell in swirling flakes as the two of them stared at each other for several minutes. Neither moving. Then after a moment she watched him get back into the taxi.

He sat a moment looking up at her staring down at him. His glanced over at his buzzing cell phone, and clenched his jaw in anger when he stared at the can of cranberry jelly, half buried under a McDonald sack. He let the cell ring until it went to voice mail. His mother would want to know when he was coming home. He was already late for dinner, and everyone would be waiting. He didn't have time to deal with the woman in the window tonight. But soon. He pounded his fist in frustration as he started the motor.

Nance watched the taxi pull out into the street. She noticed the number. The same number she had written earlier. The number she had given the detective. The taxi must have just circled the block and came back.

She wished he had come back for her, had crossed the street.

Wished he had climbed the stairs above the

Bakery and tried to find which door he could break down to reach her. Nance patted the left pocket of her slacks, like she had done a hundred times a day since she had returned home, and felt the outline of the gun. Her hand brushed over the welt across her bald head as she gazed at her reflection of the scared woman in the glass.

She wondered if she could have actually pulled the trigger. Actually killed him. She liked the idea of him being gone. Dead like all those other women he had killed, but she didn't know if she could do it.

Pull the trigger.

Not on Christmas Eve. . .but then again. . .maybe . . .

# About the Authors

The three Southern Oregon authors are busy working on their current novels.

Jennifer U. Egan is working on a YA novel, 'Globaphobia' (Fear of Balloons)

G.Z. Hill (Geri) is working on a mystery, 'The Last Vacation', set on the Oregon Coast.

Stephanie Raffelock is writing a thriller about the overturn of Roe V Wade. She produces teaching events for authors at www.novelintensives.com.

For more information on works published and soon to be released projects, the authors can be contacted at the following:

Jennifer U. Egan: eganjenni@gmail.com

G.Z. Hill: gzhglassturtle@yahoo.com

Stephanie Raffelock:

Stephanie@novelintensives.com